DEEP B

A Cam Derringer Tropical Adventure Novel

BY

MAC FORTNER

Published by TAN TOES PUBLISHING
Copyright 2022
All Rights Reserved
Edited by KEN DARROW MA
Cover design by MAC FORTNER

DEDICATION

I'd like to thank my Mother and Father for taking my sister and me to Key West when I was thirteen. It was my first tase of Florida. The drive through the Keys pulled me into a imaginative world I didn't know existed. I was captivated by the tropical landscape and always knew I would return some day.

I visit as often as I can and still plan to make it my home one day.

Watching the sunset from a tropical isle,
beats the snow by a country mile.
−Mac Fortner

BOOKS BY MAC FORTNER
CAM DERRINGER SERIES:

FREE NOVELA:
A DARK NIGHT IN KEY WEST
KNEE DEEP
BLOODSHOT
KEY WEST: TWO BIRDS, ONE STONE
MURDER FEST KEY WEST
HEMMINGWAY'S TREASURE
SAME OLD SONG
THE BAHAMA BLUES
THE WRONG KEY
LOOSE LIPS SINK SHIPS
WATER, WATER EVERYWHERE
DEEP BLUE ALIBI
DEEP BLUE DECEPTION

SUNNY RAY SERIES:

RUM CITY BAR
BATTLE FOR RUMORA

(COMING SOON)
THE SOVEREIGN SISTER

DEEP BLUE ALIBI
PROLOGUE

I was standing at a window looking out on Key West after just saving my girlfriend, Kailey, from certain death. "I wonder where that son of a bitch went," I said.

Then I felt my knees buckle, and I fell to the floor. The next thing I remember, I was floating over Kailey, Diane, Malinda, and Jack. They were crying. I felt myself slipping away from them, and then, with a rush, I was back in my body with bright lights and doctors standing around me.

"Mister Derringer, open your eyes."

I did. Standing over me was John Bexley, pointing a gun at my face. There was a loud explosion, and I jumped up.

I was on the deck of my boat, *The Same Old Song*. I was soaked in sweat, and it was the same nightmare I'd had for two months.

I closed my eyes and went back to sleep.

Stan Whittle watched through his binoculars while Cam Derringer slept in his chaise longue. He looked just like the picture in the newspaper had portrayed him two weeks ago. He looked into his rearview mirror at himself. *Almost identical. If I lose the beard, no one will know from a distance.*

He lay down the binoculars and picked his gun up from his car seat. He checked the magazine one more time.

A girl was standing behind Cam when he looked back at the boat. He lifted the binoculars to his eyes again. *Wow, what have we here?*

I was sitting on the upper deck of *The Same Old Song,* watching in astonishment. Walter had learned a new trick. I had never worked with him on this, and I had no idea where he had learned it. But there it was. He was perched on his butt, sitting straight up and staring at me.

"Walter, where did you learn that trick?"

He smiled but didn't say anything. That's when I realized he was as bored as I was.

"So you're going to learn new tricks, huh? That one's not bad, but can you go to the bar and mix me a drink?"

He cocked his head and looked at the bar. *Shit, is he thinking about it?*

I pulled my hat down to shade my eyes and closed them. If I pretended to be asleep, maybe he'd lie down.

I didn't have to pretend. Something woke me an hour later and I sat up. The first thing I saw was Walter standing about five feet away, looking at me. The second thing I saw was a mixed drink on the table next to me. *What the hell?*

He couldn't have. "Walter?"

"Talkin' to your dog again?" someone said from behind me.

I turned to see Stacy standing there in her bikini, if you can call it that. She was holding a drink in her hand. "I fixed you one," she said, looking at the drink on my table.

Thank God.

"It must be nice to just lie around all day," she said as she sat down on the chaise longue with me.

"I just sat down here no more than five minutes ago. I've been washing the boat," I replied. "Before that, I ran five miles."

She just smiled and shook her head. "That ship has sailed, Cam."

"Really? Would you like to go with me next time?"

"And be your nurse? No way," she said and laughed.

I laughed too. I knew she was jerkin' my chain.

"What's up?" I asked.

"I'm bored. I want someone to play with."

"Are you off today?"

"Yep, but Barbi has to work."

I looked at my watch—ten forty-five.

"Do you wanna start those diving lessons today?" I asked her. She'd been wanting to give it a try.

Her eyes lit up. "Hell yeah," she said.

"Is that your first drink?"

"Yes."

"Pour it out. We set sail in one hour. I'll get the tanks ready, and we'll go out to Sunset Key. We can walk out from the beach, and you can learn to sit on the bottom and breathe. I'll give you some study material for tonight, and we'll pick it back up tomorrow."

She was excited. She jumped up and poured her drink down the sink.

"Hey, watch this," I said.

"What?"

"Walter, sit up," I said and raised my hands to help him understand. He lay down. "Come on, boy, sit up." Nothing.

"Sure, Cam," Stacy said.

"Really, he did a while ago."

"You know what they say about old dogs, Cam. Can't teach 'em."

Walter is the weirdest dog I've ever seen. He'll do anything to make me look bad.

"Can we take Walter and Hank with us?" Stacy asked.

I thought about the last time I took them and they got me into a lot of trouble.

"I don't know if that would be a good idea," I said.

"Please. I'll watch 'em."

I learned long ago that I can't turn Stacy down for anything she wants. She's been good company for me on lonely nights and nursed me last month when I was shot. She's thirty-two compared to my fifty-three. We are not intimate and never will be.

Walter stood and wagged his tail, looking from her to me and back again.

"Okay," I said. "You can start by taking him down to the 'area' while I get the skiff ready."

She leaned over and kissed me on the lips. "Thanks."

"You might not be thanking me later," I said.

"Come on, Walter," she said, standing.

He wagged his whole body and ran to the steps leading down to the fantail. He stopped and looked back. When he saw Stacy walking his way, he ran down the steps. I could hear him pulling his leash off the hook.

The boat is a sleek twenty-six-foot Carolina Skiff. With its eight-inch draft, we can go anywhere in it, and the 300 h.p. engine will get us there quickly.

It actually belongs to my daughter, Diane, but I can use it whenever I want. Diane and Jack, my partner and her boyfriend, were in New England that week on vacation.

I busied myself loading the essentials. Sandwiches, water, and cookies. Then I placed Walter's water bowl and some dog food, which I knew we wouldn't need; he'd get plenty of food if we decided to make a stop.

Maybe this would take my mind off Bexley.

Stan made his call. "You were right," he said. I do look a lot like him. When he stood, he was even tall like me. Get John down to Marathon and I'll take care of the rest. While you're at it, send Holly along with him. I think I can pass her off as Cam's companion. I'll find the right targets and check his schedule."

Chapter 1

An hour later, Stacy and I left our happy home at Blue Harbour Point, slip 8, for another adventure we never foresaw.

We slipped out of the harbor and into the crystal blue waters of the Gulf of Mexico. We worked our way through Fleming Cut where we stopped and had the tanks filled at Barnacle Jill's Dive Shop. Then we headed toward Wisteria Island. We skirted the island and cruised towards Sunset Key.

As soon as I skidded onto the beach, Walter was out of the boat and running as hard as he could for who knew where followed by Hank. I had an idea though. There's a great little restaurant that way about a half-mile where the chef, Amy Roads, will give Walter anything he wants. We watched them run as we were checking our gear.

"Crabbies?" Stacy asked.

"Yep. They'll be back before we're ready to leave."

We sat in the sand as I fitted Stacy with her gear. I explained what every piece of equipment was for as I fit it to her.

"Today, we're only going to get you equipped and let you get comfortable breathing underwater. I won't be more than a foot away from you at any time and if you feel panicked, stand up."

"I'm not a baby, Cam. I'll be alright."

"I know, I'm just saying."

I've seen some pretty confident people panic as soon as they slid under the surface. I hoped Stacy wasn't one of them. And she wasn't.

We put on our flippers and backed into the water. When we were chest high, I tossed a diving buoy out and fastened it to my belt just in case another boat approached. I pointed down. She sat on the bottom and I came down beside her. She sat still for about a minute then looked at me and gave me a thumbs up, meaning she was good.

She rolled to her knees and pushed off. I went beside her. She was eager to explore the world underwater.

We swam in circles along the beach. I never let her get in over her head. I wanted her to be able to stand if needed.

A bright blue-and-yellow angel fish swam to Stacy for a brief visit. When it swam away, she looked at me wide-eyed. She was going to take to the water just fine.

We swam around for another twenty minutes. I was amazed at the way she had adapted. I looked at my gauge and instructed her to do the same. She held up one finger then five to indicate she had fifteen minutes left on the tank. I nodded since it coincided with mine.

I guided her back to our boat and pointed up. We surfaced.

She removed her mask and said, "We still have ten minutes."

"Yes, we do, but I like to be able to blow the tanks out good before we put them away. They'll last longer. You always want to take care of your gear. It's your lifeline."

I showed her how to do it and watched as she did hers. Perfect.

"That was great," she said and hugged me.

"You did good, girl. You're going to be a natural."

I looked down the beach expecting to see Walter running our way.

"Wonder where they are," Stacy said.

"No telling. Let's get these tanks in the boat, then we'll look for 'em."

As I swung my tank over the side I had to stop to keep from hitting Walter. He was lying on the deck with a big bone between his paws. Sound asleep. Hank was in a similar position on the rear seat.

"There ya go, Stacy. He always finds food. No telling what he ate before they gave him the bone. Now Hank is an accomplice."

We returned to Blue Harbour Point, docked, and unloaded the boat. I showed her where I kept the gear, how I wipe it down, and cleane the gauges.

I gave her the books and asked her to read up on all the rules of diving along with making herself familiar with the terminology.

She kissed me again, said thanks, and ran back to her boat. She was eager to get cracking on the books. Halfway there she turned and came back. "I almost forgot Hank."

We walked back to the skiff where Walter was still sound asleep. *What had they fed him?*

Hank was awake and looking dazed. When Stacy called him, he got up and followed her slowly back to her boat.

"Come on, boy," I said to Walter. One eye opened and he licked his bone.

He pulled the bone into his mouth and rolled onto his back. He closed his eye again and went back to sleep. I decided he'd come to *The Same Old Song* when he was ready, so I left him there.

When I returned to the boat, I saw Andy Prescott fishing at the end of the dock. I walked down to where he had his portable stool and tackle box set up.

"Any luck?" I asked before I got too close. I didn't want to startle him. Andy is a little slow. He fell out of a car when he was twelve. He can function fine but sometimes gets a little confused.

He turned and smiled his toothy grin. Andy is about twenty-five, tall, and lanky with a thick crop of red hair sticking out from under a Marlins ball cap. Born and raised a true conch.

"A few," he said. "Threw 'em back. Waitin' fer the biggin."

"You'll get 'im," I said turning to leave.

"Saw a guy."

I stopped and turned back to him.

"Saw a guy?" I asked.

"Snoopin."

"Where?"

"Around your boat."

I glanced back at my boat.

"On board?"

"Nah."

"What did he look like?"

"You. He stopped and looked at Stacy's boat too."

"Anything else?"

"Nah, just snoopin'."

"Thanks," I said and walked back to the boat.

I get a few people who like to walk the docks and look at the boats. Mostly just tourists who have found their way here. They think everything in Key West was placed here for their enjoyment.

Nothing on the boat seemed to be touched, so I forgot about the guy.

Stan made a note in his book. The time and date Cam had left on the skiff and the woman who had joined him. They had been diving. He watched them unload the tanks and stow them in the big boat. He wrote *Same Old Song* in his notebook again even though he already had the name of the boat.

I hope they stick to a diving schedule. It will make life a lot easier.

Chapter 2

Two months ago, I was shot in the chest by a CIA agent who was taking over the cartel in Bermuda. I was actually dead for two minutes. How I got messed up in all that still puzzles me, but I did. After some healing time, my girlfriend, ex-wife, daughter, and I set sail for Bermuda again to find the man responsible. When we arrived, Camata, the leader before the coup, was in charge again along with his new partner, John Bexley, the man who shot me. John was nowhere to be found when we arrived.

I had a bad feeling our paths would cross again. I had nightmares about him and Camata. I knew they both wanted me dead. However, Camata's hands were tied. Brittany, my ex-wife, told him she would cut his head off if anything happened to me. He believed her, and she would. She holds all the power of the Caribbean. But he is vengeful. It didn't help any that I shot him in the shoulder.

Now I'm just trying to lie back and enjoy the Key West I fell in love with as a child. Today, being with Stacy has brought back some of my zest for life.

Kailey, my girlfriend, is somewhere in Asia on assignment, I think. I only go by what she tells me, which most of the time isn't accurate, but she always seems to know what I'm doing while she's gone. She and my ex-wife are both assassins for a government hit squad called Justice. It's no wonder I can find danger at the drop of a hat.

Now I feel like going to some of my old haunts. My wounds have healed nicely and I'm strong once again. I went to the skiff again to check on Walter. He hadn't moved.

"Walter!"

He jerked and looked at me. The bone fell out of his mouth and he looked at it as if he'd never seen it before.

"Come on!"

He rose, grabbed the bone after sniffing it a moment, and jumped onto the dock. He followed me to the boat and entered when I opened the door. He went straight for the sofa and made himself comfy.

"I'll be back," I said, but he was already asleep.

I half walked and half jogged to Gary's Crab Shack and took a stool on the sidewalk. Gary came out to say, "Hi," and set a Wild Turkey on the rocks on my table.

"Glad to see ya out and about, Cam."

"Thanks, Gary. It's good to be out again. I think it's time to start life over."

"Yeah, that was a close one last time. Are ya givin' it up?"

"The PI business?"

"Yeah."

"Probably not. I wasn't even lookin' for a case when the last one found me."

"You need new friends. The ones you run with are too dangerous."

"Yes they are, but I love 'em," I said and took a sip of my drink.

"Want some legs?" he asked.

"You bet."

"I'll be right back."

While Gary was gone three more stools filled up outside. It's a local bar off the main drag, but plenty of tourists find it too.

Stan sat three stools from Cam and watched him with small, quick glances.

A waitress came outside and took his order along with another couple who had sat down.

Stan wanted to hear Cam's conversation more than watch his movements, although he did need to know his mannerisms too.

A large man came out and sat down with Cam. He brought a plate heaped with crab legs with him. They both started in on them, talking between bites.

"What's given you the new lease on life?" the man asked.

"I started giving Stacy diving lessons today. Just seeing her excitement reminded me that there are a lot of things to get excited about. Don't let life pass ya up."

"I have been tellin' you that for years, Cam."

"Really, Gary, I don't recall."

The waitress set a Bud Light down in front of Gary and another Wild Turkey in front of Cam.

"Cheers," Cam said and they clinked drinks.

"You gonna give 'er a lesson every day?"

"On her days off. Next week, she's off three days in a row. She's a quick study. It shouldn't take long."

"She's easy to look at too," Gary said and chuckled.

"She's that too."

Stan decided he'd be ready next week. Now he just had to get all the players in place.

I finished my crab legs and tried to pay, but Gary insisted this was his contribution to my new lease on life.

I thanked him and walked down to Sloppy Joe's. There were no ships in, but the walks were crowded anyway. I found a seat at the bar. Tonya placed a Wild Turkey in front of me as soon as I sat.

"Thank you and this is my last one," I said.

She kissed me on the cheek and continued her round with her tray.

I turned around on the stool so I could watch the crowd while I drank. I was also a little leery about having my back to the door.

I realized how much I have missed having Diane with me. She would always tell me when I had too much, or not enough, or if it was time to get out of here. She could sense danger in the air.

Jack is a lucky man. As long as he treats her well.

Tanya came back and squeezed between my legs. "You look lonesome, Cam."

"I am."

"Want me to come over tonight?"

"You know better than that, Tanya."

"You don't know what you're missing."

"I could imagine."

The bartender called her. "See ya later," she said and hurried off.

I sat a while and had a tall glass of water. I didn't want the day to turn into a drunken fest. Some have lately.

While I was sitting at the bar, I saw a tall man enter. He was the same man from Gary's Crab Shack. He glanced my way but kept moving and took a table for two along the wall. I didn't pay any more attention to him.

My cell rang. I looked at the caller ID. It was a strange overseas number, but I knew it was probably Kailey.

Leaving my water on the bar, I went out the side door to answer.

"Cam Derringer," I answered.

"Hot chick here," came Kailey's reply.

"Yes, you are. Is everything okay?"

"Good here. I was calling to make sure you were still healing the way you are supposed to and not out barhoppin'."

"I'm being a good boy," I said sheepishly.

"Sounds like you're in a crowd."

"Duval Street."

"Don't forget to eat."

"When are you coming home?"

"Next week, hopefully. I miss you."

"Yeah, me too."

"Who's keepin' ya busy with Diane and Jack gone?"

"Mostly Stacy. I started giving her diving lessons today."

"That's good. For both of you."

"Yes, it is. I feel alive again."

"You are alive again. I gotta go. Tell Tanya hey."

"Will do. Love ya."

"Love ya too."

We disconnected and I looked around the room. She knew I was at Sloppy Joe's when she called. She always knows where I am. *Could it be the bearded guy from Gary's and now here?*

I glanced at his table. He was gone.

Chapter 3

I went back to my boat since there was no one to play with. Stacy was sitting on her lanai reading the books I gave her.

She looked up as I passed. "You ready to go again?" she called.

"Not today. You need to study first."

"Tomorrow morning? I don't go to work until two."

I thought about it a second. "Sure, but no more than we did today. Next week, I'll start takin' ya to some diving sites."

"Yeah!" she screamed.

"You goin' out with Ryan tonight?"

"No, he's workin'."

"Steaks at six," I said and walked to my boat.

"I'll be there," she called.

When I opened the door to the boat, Walter was waiting. He seemed to have come back to life now. He was wagging and jumping. I took his leash and snapped it to his collar. He pulled me down the dock to his favorite area. I let him run and investigate for a few minutes then cleaned up behind him.

"Wanna walk a little?" I asked him.

He did and pulled me up the ramp in the parking lot and out onto the street.

Though he was itching to run, I was still recovering from my gunshot wound. This one was worse than the others. I had run daily for the last three weeks but at a slow jog.

He seemed to understand that and cut me some slack.

Stan's cell rang. "Hello," he answered.

"Okay, here's the deal. John Bexley will be arriving at Marathon Airport with Holly tomorrow evening at six-fifteen. They will check into the Isla Bella Beach Resort upon arrival. He and Holly will check in separately so no one will know they are together. Holly will contact you."

"That sounds good. Will she be bringing my money?"

"You'll get your money."

"Half up front or no go. You know how vengeful I can be."

"The money isn't a problem. Just don't screw this up. I only have one chance at this and it must be done right."

Stan hung up and smiled. *It would be good to spend a little time with Holly before we start the massacre. She'll pass as Cam's girlfriend, Stacy, just fine.*

Stan laid his phone on the seat of his car and picked up the binoculars again. Cam seemed to be favoring his right side a little. A move that would be easy to copy and add some credibility to the witnesses' statements.

When we returned to the boat, we were both getting tired. I realized I was going to have to start my recovery process by turning up the heat a little. The next day, I would start back at the gym.

I showered and lit the green egg at five-thirty. The steaks were marinating and the potatoes were in the oven.

I fixed a drink and sat at the table on the upper deck. The humid air made me sweat again, but it felt good.

I shucked my clean shirt and lay back in the chaise longue. My scar was healing fine on the outside, but it was the inside I was most worried about. I knew the doctors did a good job, but the scar I was worried about was mental. Was I going to be able to be the man I was before? I thought I would be. It was just that it was a close call this time.

"Sexy," I heard Stacy say from behind me.

She came around my chair and smiled at me.

"I meant to have my shirt back on before you arrived," I said.

She was dressed in a conservative red top and white shorts. It was probably the most covered up I've ever seen her. She was barefoot.

"You sure look beautiful this evening," I said as I slipped my shirt on.

"I wanted to dress for the dinner party."

I could tell she had spent some time with her hair and make-up. She did look beautiful.

"Join me?" I offered, holding my glass up and moving to the bar.

"Cab, please."

I opened a bottle of Cabernet and poured her one.

"Thank you," she said as I handed it to her.

I looked at her. "Okay, what's up?"

"What do you mean?"

"Well, you're all dolled up. You're being way more polite to me than you have ever been and you smell good."

She giggled. "I just want you to know how much I really do appreciate you. I loved the diving lesson today and when I was looking back on it, I realized how much you are in my life. If not for you, I probably wouldn't have made it here in Key West. I always feel safe with you around."

"Safe?" I emphasized. "I've gotten you in more trouble than any other girl on the island, except maybe Diane."

"But you always manage to save me. My life is never boring."

I held up my glass. "To never being bored."

We sat and talked the way I do with Diane. This was a different Stacy. I liked her.

"When are you going home to see your parents?" I asked her.

"Next month. I'll be gone for two weeks. Will you be okay without me?"

I smiled. "I'll miss you."

We stared at each other silently. Too silently. I was starting to get uncomfortable.

"I'll put the steaks on," I said as I stood.

"I'll check the potatoes," she said, standing too.

Bad timing for both of us. Now we were standing, facing each other, and only a foot apart. Awkward.

I chuckled nervously and stepped around her. I'd never been nervous around her before. *Snap out of it, Cam.*

"The potatoes are ready," she called from the kitchen.

"Give me five minutes," I said back to her.

She set the table and pulled the potatoes out of the oven. By the time she was ready, the steaks were too.

The evening was showing signs of becoming another beautiful sunset. The sky was orange and pink and reflected off the water. I've seen thousands of these and it's always as though it's my first.

We both stopped eating and watched the sky for a minute. "Nice, huh?" I said.

"Fantastic."

We continued to eat.

"What time tomorrow?" I asked her to give her the chance to get some sleep before she had to go to work.

"Can you be up by six?"

"I'll be waiting for you." I said.

"Where will we go?"

"I've been thinking about that. How about we go to Fort Zackery Taylor?"

"Cool, where to next time?"

"Joe's Tug."

"Where's that?"

"South about seven miles. Not too far from here. It's a beautiful dive. I think you'll love it."

"That sounds great to me," she said, getting her young girl's excitement back.

"Good, the depth is ten to fifty feet. It'll be perfect for you. Then I have some other sites in mind for the rest of the week. By next weekend, you'll be certified and a real diver."

She didn't say anything. She just stared at the sunset with a huge grin on her face. Her eyes sparkled in the reflection of the sky.

I returned to my steak.

When we'd finished, we cleared the table and had one more nightcap.

"Thanks for the evening, Cam," she said. "It's nice to spend some time, just the two of us."

"Yes, it is, Stacy. We're usually rushed when we're together. I feel I know you better now."

"Do you like me?"

"Yes, I do. As a matter of a fact, I love you."

"Thanks, I love you too."

I stood and said, "Now, you need to get to bed and be ready for what tomorrow holds. No more drinking tonight."

She stood and saluted me. "Aye, aye, sir."

I hugged her and kissed her on the cheek. "See you in the morning."

"Okay, she said and left the boat.

I watched her until she stepped onto her boat. She turned and looked back catching me watching her. She smiled and waved.

Chapter 4

At six-twenty-five the following evening, Stan watched from a bench in the Marathon airport as Holly and John Bexley waited for their luggage.

Holly glanced at him and showed the hint of a smile at the corner of her lips then looked away.

He snapped a quick photo of Bexley then turned his attention away from them. Now with the picture of his target and the bug he planted on Cam's boat today while he was gone, his plan had a route.

The search he put out on a skiff that matched Cam's had brought in two results already. He would pick one up in Marathon the following day and have the name and numbers changed to match.

With the bug planted, he heard Cam and Stacy talking when they returned from their dive. Stacy would work tomorrow and then be off for three days. They were going to get in all the diving they could. In two days, they would go to Joe's Tug to spend the day diving. It was seven miles south of Key West. They would probably be there alone. To make sure, he had hired an acquaintance, Lance Peters, from Key Largo to shadow them and scare off any other divers that might be in the area.

Things would move fast, but that was the way he liked it. Stan rose and left the airport. He had details to attend to. The first was to find the perfect kill sight.

I was feeding Walter when I heard more than felt someone step onto the boat. I looked out the sliding door and saw Andy Prescott standing on my lanai.

I opened the door and stepped out. "Andy, how are you?"

"Good," he said. "Saw a man."

We had already had this conversation a few days ago. "Again?" I asked.

"Yep."

"Where?"

"On this boat."

"Actually on the boat?"

"Yep."

"What was he doing?"

"Snooping."

"What did he look like?"

"You."

Andy gets confused easily. My first thought was that he saw me on the boat earlier and thought it was someone who looked like me. That wouldn't be such a stretch.

"Thank you, Andy. I'll have security keep a watch out for him."

"Okay," he said and turned to go.

"Would you like a Coke and something to eat?" I asked.

"No, thank you. I got a big one today," he said and pointed at a bucket on the dock. "Gonna eat it fresh."

"You're a lucky man, Andy. Enjoy."

"Yes, sir, Cam."

He stepped onto the dock, lifted his bucket, and left.

I thought about the man he said he saw on my boat. What if someone *was* snooping around? Who would it be?

I decided to check my surveillance cameras. I didn't think I'd reset them since the storm I was caught in at sea a few months ago.

I removed the back panel behind the controls for the camera. I was right. The wires were fried from a lightning strike.

I pulled the wiring out as far as it would come. This was not going to be repairable. I knew I should have fixed it right away, but I was in the hospital for a few days and then on the mend. Kailey, Malinda, and Diane took all of my time spoiling me. Then Stacy took over when we returned from Bermuda. I am a lucky man to have such women in my life.

"Walter, do you wanna go to the Home Depot with me?"

He sat up looking excited. It didn't matter where we were going to him. He just wanted to go. There would more than likely be food or treats involved.

I grabbed my wallet and told Walter to get his leash. He pulled it off the hook and carried it to the parking lot beside me.

The Home Depot wasn't overly crowded so I snapped the leash on Walter and he entered the store with me. He was immediately discovered by a group of teenage girls who petted him vigorously. He squinted and smiled at me.

Yeah, I remember those days, I thought.

I dragged him away and found the security section where I picked out a wireless camera and a few alarms to fasten to it. It would work nicely for what I needed.

On the way home, I stopped at Jimmy's Burger Hut and got us each a burger. We sat in the car and ate while we watched the tourists. Walter's was gone in a matter of seconds. Then he stared at mine.

"Sorry, old boy. I've told you a million times to eat slowly."

His attention turned to the bag. He stuck his snout down inside. When he looked back up, the bag was stuck over his head. He ignored it. He sat in the seat and looked around as if it wasn't even there.

"You are weird," I said.

A couple walking through the lot stopped and pointed at him. He looked toward them. The girl pulled out her phone and snapped a picture of him. They laughed and walked away looking at the picture.

"Doesn't that embarrass you even a little?" I asked him.

He looked at me with Jimmy's Burger Hut in big red letters wrapped around his head. I noticed the bag was moving with his breath. I didn't want him to hyperventilate so I pulled the bag off his head and dropped my wrapper in it. He smiled.

We went back to the boat to install the new system.

Stan drove around the island then left it on the North Overseas Highway. Marathon was a little too crowded, but the surrounding area would make for an easy getaway and still have some witnesses to the shooting.

After checking Duck Key and Key Colony, he realized he wasn't going to get the initial reaction he was looking for. He returned to Marathon and drove to the south side. When he came to Sombrero Beach, he knew he had found the perfect spot. There were always tourists there and the water made for an easy escape.

He could get to Key West and make his getaway before he was discovered. This would be perfect. He walked around the park and took in the sights. It was an interesting area.

Some sailboats held Stan's interest for a few minutes. There was a beautiful park and beach. This would be the spot where it would all come together.

He stood on the beach for a bit and pictured the charge, shooting, and getaway. He smiled to himself. His concentration was broken by the sound of children to his right. Three small boys and what was probably their little sister were running toward the water across the beach.

I hope they're not here on D-Day.

Stan sat on the edge of a picnic table and thought back to his childhood. He had one brother and a sister, but he didn't remember their father ever taking them to a beach in Cleveland.

These kids look happy. They have big smiles on their faces. They're full of life.

Stan's own life was quite the opposite. His father would come home drunk and beat him and his brother. Then he would take his sister to the bedroom. He could still hear her screams.

He finally fell in with some of the boys from the neighborhood who had bad home lives too. All of their fathers were friends. They drank together almost every night. Sometimes they would trade daughters for a night.

One day, while the boys were planning how to rob a drugstore, one of the them, Jake Logan, said, "If my father finds out I did that, he'll take my money then kill me."

Stan knew Jake's father. He probably would do just that. That's when they made the pact. "Our fathers will never hurt us again," Stan had said. "It stops now."

"How?" Elliot, the other boy, asked.

"We kill them," Stan said coldly.

The boys all looked at each other wide-eyed. Finally, Stan held his hand in the air. The others clasped his hand one at a time. "We will be known as the Marshals," Stan said. "What we do will be justified."

They broke their grip and cheered. Over the next year, the boys' fathers died one at a time. One was from a robbery gone bad and one was a car accident even though the mechanic at the impound garage said the brake line had been cut. Another's father was shot in the head while lying in a park passed out. No blame was ever directed toward the boys, but they were the ones who did it.

Their lives were better afterward, but they had the taste of blood in them. They did little odd jobs for a local gang. They would beat someone up or watch for the police while the gang would rob a store. Mostly small stuff that only fed their appetite for something more.

Then, one morning, Stan got word that Jake and Elliot were killed the night before. They had tried to rob a man sitting in his car. He was a cop and shot them both point-blank.

Stan staked out the policeman's house and waited. Four days later, when the cop returned home after his second shift, Stan walked up to him in his front yard and said, "You killed my friends." He raised his gun and shot the officer in the forehead.

Stan hot-wired a car two blocks away and drove to Chicago where he found another gang to fall in with. Eventually, he was taking odd jobs. Mostly as an assassin. It paid well and he was good at it. He didn't care whom he killed. They were all just targets.

Now at fifty-five, he was one of the top paid assassins in the world. The job he was currently on would pay one million dollars. The Camata cartel had a bottomless checkbook. The catch was that he had to make it look as if Cam Derringer was the assassin.

The little girl's scream broke his thoughts. The boys were splashing her with water. Their mother ran to them and told them to stop. They did.

Stan searched the area for a camera. There was one on a pole close to the beach and one on a wall near the center of the picnic area. He would make sure they caught him and his bloody carnage.

Now he needed to get back to his hotel and wait for Holly to call.

Chapter 5

The new system was installed in fifteen minutes. No wires attached. Things sure are easier nowadays. I connected the Bluetooth to my phone and laptop. While I was checking it a blur came onto the screen. It was moving and getting worse. I went back inside to the camera. Walter was licking the lens.

"Walter! Stop!"

He looked at me for a second then returned to licking. Well, I was going to have to locate it high enough that he couldn't reach it.

I decided on a good spot on the lanai. It would be covered from the weather and pick up any activity on the deck. Now I was thinking about picking up a second camera for inside.

My phone rang. It was Diane.

"Hello baby," I answered.

"Hey, Dad. What ya doin'?"

"Installing a new security system on my boat. The other one was fried from the storm we were in a few months ago."

"Oh, yeah, that was a bad one."

"Everything okay there?"

"It's great here. We're having a blast, but I feel guilty leaving you there all alone."

"I'm not alone. Stacy has been keeping me quite busy with her diving lessons."

"Is she catching on?"

"She was born to dive."

"Great. I miss it myself."

"We'll all go when you get back."

"I'm lookin' forward to it."

"Okay, just have fun and don't worry about me. I can't get in too much trouble in one week. Tell Jack I said, 'Hey.'"

She paused a minute. "Jack wants to talk to ya."

"Put him on."

"Hey, Cam. Did I hear you say you were installing a new security system?"

"Yep, wireless."

"Good. What would you think about sending the signal to my phone too?"

"So you can watch me all the time? No way."

"No. I promise I won't turn it on except in an emergency. As a matter of fact, you can control when it's on."

"Well, I guess I could do that. I'll just turn yours on when I'm not home."

Jack gave me instructions on how to set it up and connect to his phone. Then he put Diane back on.

"Thanks, Dad. I feel a lot better now."

"You have to quit worrying about me," I said.

"I know. I can't help it. You're always getting into some kind of trouble."

"Those days are over."

"Sure they are, Cam."

"You two enjoy."

"Will do. Love ya."

"Love you too."

After we hung up I turned off Jack's access. That was probably a good idea to have them hooked up.

I walked back inside where Walter was sitting up again in the center of the galley.

"What do you want now?"

He looked at his food bowl and back at me. His water bowl was missing as usual. I put some dog food in his bowl and went in search of his water bowl. One good thing about the new security was that when he hid his bowl, I'd be able to watch where he put it. I found it in the head in the master stateroom.

After I filled it, I thought about how strange he'd been acting. Did he think I was lonesome and needed to be entertained or was he just getting bored with me and was missing Diane and Kailey?

Either way, he was definitely entertaining.

I patted him on the head and said, "I'll be back."

I grabbed my keys and left. I wanted to be around some humans who would talk to me for a while.

"Where ya goin'?" Stacy asked from her boat as I passed.

"Not sure. Maybe Hog's Breath. Wanna go?"

She jumped up and said, "Give me a sec."

She disappeared inside and returned dressed in red shorts and a white blouse.

"This okay?" she asked, posing for me.

"Perfect," I said.

Our flip-flops kept a steady beat on the wooden dock as we walked to the parking lot. When we got in the car, I remembered the security system.

I pulled out my phone and turned on Jack's feed.

"What's that?"

I explained it to her.

"I want one."

"I'll get you one tomorrow. When you get home from work, it'll be installed."

"Cool."

We found a spot to park three blocks from the bar. We were actually closer to Captain Tony's and decided to stop there for a drink.

We grabbed two stools at the bar. The bartender came to us and said, "Shit, Cam. How do you get all these young girls? Each one is prettier than the last."

I just smiled and shrugged.

Stacy said, "He's the best lover in Key West. We all want him," as she rubbed my shoulder.

"You haven't even givin me a chance," he said.

"I've heard about you, Jimmy," Stacy said.

"Huh," he said, knowing he wasn't going to win this one. "What ya drinkin'?"

He brought us two Wild Turkeys.

Stan and Holly lay on the floor laughing. The sheets were wrapped around them still half on the bed where they had started.

Between deep breaths, Holly said, "You must have missed me."

"I don't think so. I believe I hit you dead center."

They laughed again.

Holly had shown up at his door twenty minutes ago looking like an innocent young college girl. They started at each other's clothes before they even said, "Hello."

Now lying on the floor, Stan said, "I have some pictures I want to show you. I want you to see Stacy. You'll be able to look enough like her to pass in all the confusion."

"Where is she?"

"Key West. She lives on a boat close to Cam."

"Should we be seen together?"

"It doesn't matter yet. As long as I have my beard, no one will be the wiser."

"I hate for you to shave it."

"I'll grow it back. Where's Bexley?"

"He was in his room when I left. He thinks he's here for a meeting with the Santana Cartel from Miami. Which he is. What he doesn't know is that Camata wants him and the two cartel members dead. Santana didn't want to meet in Bermuda and Camata didn't want to meet in Miami, so they decided on Marathon.

"John wants to go to Key West too. He was disappointed that Cam didn't die two months ago when he shot him."

"He'll be in for a surprise when Cam kills him instead," Stan said. "I have the perfect spot. I want you to have John meet them at Sombrero Beach. They wanted something secluded."

"Camata is sure going to a lot of trouble just so he isn't connected to Cam's death."

"That's how afraid he is of Brittany. She'll destroy anyone who harms Cam."

"She sounds dangerous."

"She is and she doesn't work alone. There's an organization behind her. Even I have been warned never to get involved with her."

"But you are now," Holly said.

"They'll never know it was me. All the blame for this one goes to Cam. He'll either get killed by the cops or go to prison for the murder of John Bexley. Camata doesn't care which as long as Cam is taken care of."

"And the girl?"

"Collateral damage. Too bad for her."

"When we go to Key West tomorrow, I want to see Stacy for myself."

"She'll be working at the Coyote Ugly. We'll stop in there."

We finished our drinks at Captain Tony's and moved down the street to Hog's Breath. There was a band playing and Stacy wanted to dance.

"Just take it easy on me," I said.

"You're milking that gunshot thing. It's time for you to start living again."

She pulled me to the dance floor. I have to admit it did feel good to move freely again. She knew what I needed.

After two songs she took mercy on me and we sat. We ordered some seafood and chased it with beer. It hit the spot.

"Are we going to dive in the morning?" Stacy asked.

"No, you go to work at ten don't you?"

"Yes."

"We have a full three days of diving after that. You need your rest tomorrow."

"I need my rest?" she asked.

"Yes, and I have a few things to do tomorrow."

"Okay, I'll let you slide."

"Are you ready?" I asked her.

"Sure," she said.

We left and walked back toward the car. Stacy looped her arm in mine. It felt good, but I was starting to worry that she might be getting a little too attached.

I looked down at her.

I think she saw the discomfort in my eyes. "Don't flatter yourself, Cam. I'm not falling for you. I just like you a lot as a friend and I like to be close to you."

"I know that," I said. "I like you a lot too."

"Besides, Kailey would kick my ass."

"And mine, I'm afraid."

It was nine-thirty before we returned to the boat. Stacy got Hank, and I went for Walter.

"See ya at our spot," she said, meaning the area where the dogs like to do their business.

I saluted her as I left.

Walter was more than eager to get there, but when he saw Hank already there he had to attack him. They rolled around a bit before they decided they needed to pee.

"Now that's the way to live," Stacy said. "Roll around in the mud then pee right in front of everyone."

I laughed. "I've never thought of living like that, but maybe it does have its appeal."

When they were finished, we went back to the dock. I bid her goodnight and went home.

Holly went to John Bexley's room at nine o'clock that night. When he answered the door, he smiled.

"I knew you couldn't stay away," he said.

"Don't get your hopes up, buddy."

"A guy can dream."

"Okay, we have the perfect spot for you to meet the cartel. I scouted the area and came up with Sombrero Beach. You can go check it out tomorrow. You drive there for the meeting and I'll come in by water. They won't be expecting me. If anything goes wrong, I'll be there to back you up."

"What can go wrong? We're just meeting to work out the details for the drug deal. Camata has already told them what he wants of them."

"Yeah, if they agree."

"They'll agree. We have the upper hand. They're trying to work their way into our territory, but we're not going to allow that. They only get what we give 'em."

When Holly left, Bexley called Rafael Camacho in Miami.

"We'll meet at Sombrero Beach in two days," John said. "Be there at nine a.m. There are plenty of people hanging around so nothing can happen."

"How do I know we can trust you?"

"Like I said, it's a crowded beach. We'll all be safe that way."

"Did you bring a sample?"

"Yeah, I got a sample. Be there," John said and hung up.

Chapter 6

The following day, I drove back to The Home Depot and bought a second camera for my system and a system for Stacy and Barbie. I left Walter at home.

The man at the store was right. The second camera hooked up to the system with no trouble. The hub controlled them both so I didn't have to reprogram Jack into it.

I caught Stacy before she left for work and told her I was going to install her alarm that day.

"Cool. Thank you so much. Leave the bill on the table."

"No charge. Just a little thanks for taking care of me."

She kissed me on the cheek. "Barbie won't be home either. She's spending a week with her boyfriend in Miami."

"Sounds like fun. Let her know I'll be there anyway. I'll take Hank out in a while."

"Thanks. See ya tomorrow."

Holly left the hotel early that morning and picked Stan up at his room. She drove him to Marathon to Overboard Marina where he examined and rented the skiff.

He told the guy he'd pick it up in an hour. Holly took him down the road to a marine shop where he bought matching numbers for the boat and a blank decal to write the name on the back. He had enough talent to copy the name for what time they would need it.

Stan picked the boat up an hour later. He unpacked his bag from the car.

"We'll change the numbers and name and then be at Garrison Bight around noon. Be sure to have John at the beach tomorrow by nine."

"I have that all figured out. He'll be there," Holly said.

"Good. I don't see any problems with the plan. Of course, anything can happen, but we'll handle it."

Holly jumped in the boat and Stan pushed away from the dock. The boat fired up and he idled out of the marina into the open waters of the Atlantic Ocean.

He found a secluded beach area at Bahia Honda Park and slid the skiff onto the sand. From his bag, he pulled the new numbers out and started to work on the side of the boat while Holly spread a towel and lay on the beach. A half-hour later, the numbers were covered to match Cam's. Now he placed the blank decal on the stern and freehanded the name *Diane's Days* onto the boat.

They pulled into Garrison Bight at twelve ten. He docked at a transient slip and tied the boat off.

"Do ya think the numbers will pass?" she asked.

"The boat is ready to go."

"Good, let's go to Coyote Ugly. I wanna see her."

"Okay, on the way I'll show you Cam's boat. Maybe he'll be there."

They rented a scooter two blocks away and rode to Blue Harbour Point and parked in the lot. Stan pointed to Cam's boat. "That's it. The one across and up two is Stacy's."

"Very nice boats," she said.

"Yeah."

Just then Cam came out with his dog.

"He's coming up here," Stan said. "Let's go."

He started the scooter and circled the lot. He pulled out of the drive and drove toward town.

They parked a half-block from Coyote Ugly and walked to the bar.

Taking a seat at a table, Stan pointed Stacy out. Their luck held. Stacy came to their table to take their order.

When she left to turn the order in, Holly smiled at Stan. "She's a real fox."

"She sure is," he said.

"I think I can pull her off," Holly said. "We'll get some of their clothing and I can make my hair look like hers with the help of a wig. You're really close to being Cam."

"Yeah, I think so. Tomorrow, I'll cut the beard."

"Sounds good. We'll watch the dock today. If Cam leaves, we'll be able to go on board and get their clothes."

"How are we going to get John to hold the meeting at Sombrero Beach?" Stan asked.

"I already told him it looked like a good spot. He's all for it."

"Perfect."

I stopped at Stacy's boat and got Hank. I took him and Walter for a short walk around the marina and then returned to Stacy's boat.

I looked around her boat for the best spot to place the camera and settled on the underside of the aft top deck. From there it would pick up part of the dock and all of her fantail.

I finished the hook-up and tested the camera running the feed to my phone. The next day I'd hook it to Stacy's.

It worked perfectly. I decided to take Hank with me today so Walter would have some company other than me.

After finding Walter's water bowl and filling it, I put it into the skiff. Walter, Hank, and I got in and slipped out of the marina and toward Barnacle Jill's Dive Shop.

"Hey, Cam."

"Hey, Jill."

"Need to fill those tanks?"

"Yeah, if you have time. All four of 'em."

"Not a problem. It'll be about a half-hour."

"I left the dogs in the boat," I told her.

"I'll bring 'em in here."

"Okay, I'll walk down to Salties and get a bite to eat. Want anything?"

"Chillie dog and fries," she said.

"You got it."

Jill is around sixty-five, would be my guess anyway. She's close to six feet tall and has a very athletic body. Her skin is brown and weathered from her many years in the sun. She told me that she started diving at the age of five and will never give it up. I guess she deserves a chili dog and fries once in a while.

Salties is a small wharf bar mostly inhabited by locals. It sits at the end of the marina where the dive shop is located. Today, it had an unusual clientele. Two of the tables were full. Five college-age girls sitting at each. I took a stool at the bar.

"What's up, Cam?" Aaron asked as he came to the bar to take my order.

"I was about to ask you the same," I said, glancing over my shoulder.

"I've been discovered by the Delta Zeta," he said, grinning. "Beats the hell out of the smelly fishermen."

"Yes, I guess it does. I'll have a fishbowl of Yuengling and a grouper sandwich. Before I leave, I need a chili dog and fries to go."

"Jill?" he asked.

"Yep."

"She never comes to see me anymore. I think I made her mad."

"What did you do now?"

"I kissed her the last time she came in."

"Kissed her?"

"I couldn't help it. She's beautiful and I might have been a little drunk."

"Every girl wants to be kissed by a drunk bartender."

"I know."

"I think you should go down there and apologize to her. Tell her you're sorry and it will never happen again."

"Unless she wants it to."

"No, I think I'd leave that part out for now. Maybe later, after you're friends again, you can work on that."

When he came back with my beer, I lifted it and took a sip. I turned sideways on my stool and surveyed the room. There were five other men in there at three tables. They were most definitely fishermen in from their morning run. They were all eyeing the girls, who were ignoring them.

I saw two of the girls talking and looking at me. One of them got up and came to my stool.

"Are you Cam Derringer?" she asked.

I was got and it probably showed on my face. I nodded.

"I did a report on you a few months ago. You saved that girl and then got shot."

"Yes, I remember doing that," I said.

"Can I take a picture with you?" she asked, holding her phone up for a selfie.

As I was about to say sure, she snapped the picture.

"Thanks," she said; then she kissed me on the cheek and returned to her table.

"What the hell, Cam," Aaron said as he set my grouper sandwich on the bar. "How'd you get her to do that?"

"I didn't get her to do anything. She recognized me from an article."

"Yeah, you're famous. I want to be famous someday."

"You will be. You'll be known as the bartender at Salties where all the schoolgirls hang out. The word'll get around. But if I were you, I'd wear a clean shirt and comb my hair."

Aaron smiled at this. "Yeah," he said.

As soon as I finished my sandwich, Aaron placed a bag on the counter. "Tell 'er I said hi, will ya?"

"I'll tell 'er, but you need to go and apologize to her, not me."

"Yeah, I will."

I returned to the dive shop and saw my tanks by the door.

"Here's your food," I said, setting the bag on the counter.

"Did Aaron fix it?"

"I don't know. He gave it to me and said to tell you, 'Hi.'"

"Puh," she muttered.

She looked into the sack and smiled. "Two chili dogs."

"I think he's trying to apologize," I said.

"Yeah, I know, but I'm going to let him suffer for a while."

"He said he kissed you because you're so beautiful he couldn't stop himself."

She blushed. "He's silly."

I could tell by the way she was acting that they would be friends again soon.

"Here's the money for the food," she said, picking up her purse.

"No charge," I said. "Thanks for watching the dogs."

"Thanks. No charge for the tanks."

"Thank you. I'll see ya soon."

I saw her opening the sack and pulling out a chili dog as I was leaving.

There are little stories all over Key West. You just have to pay attention.

Chapter 7

I left the dive shop and decided to cruise around Key West, taking the long way home. The water was smooth and the sun bright. I removed my shirt to let the fresh air get to my wounds. The heat and humidity felt good on my skin. The wind from the speed of the boat dried it immediately.

My phone beeped as I was passing Smathers Beach. I stopped the boat, pulled my phone out, and checked the screen.

It had captured a short video from Stacy's boat. I ran it and saw Andy Prescott walking toward the end of the dock. He was carrying a fishing pole and tackle box. He had a bucket secured with a rope over his shoulder. When he disappeared, the movie stopped running.

I smiled to myself. *This is what we've needed for a long time. I'll feel better about leaving the boat unattended while I'm out and about.*

The phone beeped again as Andy passed my boat. *Tomorrow, I'll take Stacy's camera off my phone and put it on hers. I don't want to spy on her.*

I turned my feed off for the time being. I'd set it all up tomorrow with a fresh start.

"They're gone," Stan said. "Let's get some clothes and get out of here."

They walked the dock to Stacy's boat. "I'll get hers. You go on to Cam's boat," Holly said.

She walked onto the forward deck and tried the door. It wasn't even locked. She slid it open and disappeared inside.

Stan was on Cam's boat now. His door was locked. He looked around and saw no one else was on the dock. He climbed the latter to the second deck. The pilot house was locked too. He didn't want to break any windows so he kept searching for a way in.

He found the hatch over the master cabin open. Easing the screen out carefully, he laid it on the deck, then dropped through the hatch landing on the bed. He stood on the bed and pulled the screen back in place.

He found some shorts and a T-shirt in the top drawer of Cam's dresser. He took them and walked through the boat to the lounge where he unlocked the door and eased his way out. He closed the door but couldn't lock it. *Cam will just think he left it unlocked.*

When Stan returned to Stacy's boat, Holly was already waiting for him with some clothing in her hands.

"Let's get out of here," Stan said.

They left the lot and drove to Garrison Bight where they jumped into the boat and pushed off.

They sped out of the marina causing a few of the fishermen to look their way.

"It'll be late when we get back to Marathon. But we'll still have time to make love again," Stan said.

"Plenty of time."

I cut up through Cow Key Channel, turned left and motored toward Trumbo Point. Normally I pull into Garrison Bight and have a few drinks with Jack. Since he was gone I turned into Blue Harbour Point and pulled up behind my boat.

It was getting late but I decided to take Walter for a short run. We both needed it. I returned Hank to his boat then Walter and I walked to the top of the parking lot; and then I started a slow and comfortable jog. Walter fell in beside me. He didn't try to pull me faster as he usually does. I think he could sense my need to work back into this.

When we returned, I was surprised to see Stacy's car in the lot. She was sitting on her patio.

"What are you doing home so early?" I asked.

"It was slow so I asked if I could leave. I thought we might be able to get out earlier tomorrow."

"That sounds good to me."

"I saw you have my camera hooked up. Does it work?"

"Yep, let me have your phone."

She handed me her phone and I redirected the feed to it and canceled mine.

"Here ya go," I said, handing her phone back to her.

I showed her how to work it while she held it. She caught on right away. It must be nice to be young.

"Thanks. I feel safer already."

"You're welcome. I feel better about you being here. So, you're anxious about tomorrow."

"I can't wait. I love being down there. Is Joe's Tug beautiful?"

"It is a 75-foot, steel-hulled shrimp boat and one of the Lower Keys' most well-known novice scuba diving wreck sites. You'll love it."

"Cool, I can't wait."

"Get some sleep," I said, pulling Walter away. "I'll see you at six."

"Love you," she called.

"Love you too."

When we stepped on board the boat, Walter ran to the door and nosed it open. I didn't remember leaving it unlocked. What good is a security system if I'm not going to lock my doors?

Three hours later, Holly and Stan were in bed at Stan's hotel. They were panting from their third round of lovemaking.

"You're going to kill me with that thing someday," Holly said.

"No way. I can hardly keep up with you anymore."

"Next time, I'll take it easy on you."

"Don't you dare." They laughed.

"I guess we'd better get some sleep. We need to get up early and make last-minute plans.

"Yep, tomorrow will be a big day," Stan said, smiling. He'd grown to love kill day.

"Will we leave Marathon right away?"

"I've chartered a plane at two. It'll take us to Miami and you have a flight to Bermuda at ten past four."

"Where will you go?"

Stan smiled at her. "No one knows."

With everything finished for the evening, I decided to turn in early. As soon as my head hit the pillow, my cell rang. It was Malinda, better known now as Brittany.

"What do you want now?" I answered.

"I just thought I'd check up on my ex-husband. I want to make sure you're healing properly."

"That I am. As a matter of fact, I've been diving with Stacy. We're going out again tomorrow."

"Great. That will be good exercise without putting too much strain on your muscles."

"Yep, now why did you call?"

"You don't think I just wanted to check up on you?"

"Oh, I believe that's part of it."

Malinda hesitated a bit then said, "I wanted you to know that John Bexley is in Marathon. He arrived two days ago. I'm sure it has something to do with one of the cartels but I'm not sure which one. My guess would be the Santana Cartel from Miami. I think Camata has been wanting to do a little business with them."

I froze for a few seconds. The man who almost killed me was only an hour away.

"Cam?" Malinda said.

"Yeah, I'm here. Does he have plans to come to Key West?"

"I don't know. That's why I wanted to give you a heads-up. I think it's a good idea for you and Stacy to go diving though. I'll try to keep track of him and let you know if he heads that way."

"Okay, I appreciate the info, but I don't think he'd come after me again. He'd know that you'd have a track on him."

"Yeah, probably, but I still want you to be careful. Either way, he doesn't have long to live. The first time he shows his face around Bermuda, he's a dead man."

"Well, until then, I'm going to live life as I see fit. Don't worry about me, I'll be fine. Do you know where he is in Marathon?"

"You don't need to know that, Cam. I don't want you to go after him. We'll take care of him before he can do anything."

"Like I said, don't worry about me. I'll be diving tomorrow."

"Okay, I just wanted to give you a heads-up. I'll talk to you tomorrow. I love you."

"Thanks for the call. I love you too. Goodnight."

I lay in bed and thought about John being so close. I wondered if he'd been closer than he was now. I got out of bed and checked the locks on my doors. I had already made the place secure. I returned to bed, but I slept restlessly. When the alarm went off at five, I jumped up startled.

Walter was standing in the doorway watching me. I shut the alarm off. "Sorry, boy. I didn't mean to scare you."

I went to the galley and switched on the coffee maker then went to the door and eased it open. I looked out to the deck.

Walter sensed I was on edge and came to my side poking his head out and looking around the deck too.

I patted his head to reassure him that everything was okay. I also reassured myself that everything was okay. It wasn't like me to be scared. Sure, I've been scared plenty of times when there was something to be scared of. But this time, I was scared of what might happen.

I shook the feeling off and poured a cup of joe. I sat on the lanai and watched the beginning of the sunrise. It promised to be a bright, sunny, hot, and humid day.

I walked to the edge of the dock and looked down it. I saw Stacy's light come on in her parlor. I called her.

"I've got some fresh coffee," I said.

"Great, I'll be right there."

A couple of minutes later, she stepped onto the boat wearing an oversized T-shirt. She plopped a white sack on the table. "I'm gonna get some coffee. You can start on one of these."

I recognized the sack. Betty's Bakery. I opened it and looked inside. Four chocolate honeybuns.

When Stacy returned, she kissed me on the cheek. "With Diane gone, I thought you might be having withdrawals."

"I was. Thank you very much."

I tore off a corner and held it out for Walter. He gently took it out of my hand and then looked at Stacy.

"Look what you started," she said, breaking off a corner of hers.

"Okay Walter, that's all," I said.

Shockingly, he walked to the door and lay down.

"Can you believe that?" Stacy said.

"He's trying a lot of new things lately. I think he's messing with me."

We ate our donuts and drank our coffee quietly watching the eastern sky turn orange.

"Well," Stacy said, "that was good. I'm gonna go get ready."

"I'll put some things on the boat and be ready in a half-hour."

"Can't wait," she said. "Can we take Hank and Walter?"

I thought about it for a beat and said, "There is a nice beach we can stop at after the dive. I think they'd like that. We'll stop there for a minute on the way out so they can do their business. They'll be fine in the boat until we finish."

"Cool."

She went back to her boat. When I stood to go in, Walter was sitting up in front of the door. I quickly looked to see if Stacy was still in viewing distance. Too late, she was gone.

I opened the door and stepped around him. Why was he so weird?

I loaded the boat and added dog food and water. We had some snacks too.

When Stacy came, she had a large bag with her. "Extra clothes," she said, "and some sandwiches."

I was glad she'd brought more clothes because she didn't have much on. "Great," I said.

Hank and Walter jumped into the boat and took their position on the bow cushions. Stacy pushed us off and sat down next to me.

We idled out of the marina and into the gulf. We turned northeast and cut through Cow Key Channel. At the end of the channel, I pulled the boat onto a sandy beach and told the dogs to get out.

Walter knew the drill. He jumped out and quickly relieved himself then jumped back in. Hank caught on and did the same.

We pushed off and headed southeast into the Atlantic Ocean.

"Here we are," I said as I pulled the throttle back. "See that marker?"

"Yeah," she said.

"It's sixty-five feet below."

I dropped the anchor.

"It looks like we're the only ones out here," Stacy said.

I looked around the horizon. "Just that boat over there," I said, pointing to a boat we passed as we entered the area. "It looks as though they're doing some testing."

Another boat came toward us but the first boat intercepted it. It turned and left the area.

"I wonder why they let us in?" Stacy asked.

"Don't know."

Chapter 8

Stan stood at the sink in the bathroom. He didn't like to do it, but he put a new blade in his razor, lathered his face, and began work on the beard. In five minutes it was gone.

Holly appeared at the bathroom door. He turned to look at her. She let out a laugh. "Oh my God. You look ten years younger."

She ran her hand over his face and then kissed him. She was falling for him again. That could not happen. *They met five years ago when they were in Colorado. She had a boyfriend who was in the marijuana business. A semi-legal business actually. Someone, she had never found out who, didn't like the competition and placed a bounty on her boyfriend's head.*

The guy needed to die anyway. He was an asshole who beat Holly for everything he did wrong. If she'd had a place to go, she would have run away. But she stayed hoping he would change his ways. Then, one day, while she was lying on the floor being kicked, her boyfriend's head exploded. She lay there in disbelief. That was when Stan walked into the room and helped her to her feet.

"Are you okay?" he had asked.

Holly nodded but was holding her stomach. It felt as if she had a broken rib. It turned out she had two.

Stan got a hotel room and stayed with Holly for three days. He didn't seem like a hitman to her. He was gentle and caring. He told her he had never hung around after a hit before but he liked her and wanted to make sure she was going to be alright.

On their last night together they made slow, gentle love. He left her five thousand dollars and told her to go home. She told him she couldn't. He understood.

"Give me your phone number," he said. She did. He called her every few days for a month; then the calls were fewer and further between.

One day, he called and said he needed her help on a job. Would she be interested in making fifty thousand dollars? That was her first hit. Now they'd worked together on six jobs and she had enjoyed every minute of it.

"Do we have time to go back to bed?" she asked, still feeling his face.

"After the job," he said.

They dressed in Cam's and Stacy's clothes. They packed their clothing in a bag and one at a time left the hotel. Stan would go get the boat and meet Holly at Porky's Bayside Restaurant. There were docks just outside the building.

She was waiting on the dock when he arrived. She stepped into the boat when he bumped the dock and pushed off with her foot. She lay on the floor out of sight until they were out of the marina.

The sun was on the horizon making the sky look as if it were on fire. Stan looked at his watch. "Three hours," he said.

"Let's go check out the beach."

"We're on the way."

They cruised to the end of the key where Stan pulled the boat onto a beach in front of the Sunset Bar and Grill.

"Go in and get us some breakfast," he told Holly. "It's time to start being seen."

"Are you ready?" I asked Stacy.

"I'm always ready," she said.

"I'm going to drop a downline," I said as I pulled it from the storage under the seat. "We probably won't need it, but I want you to get familiar with it."

I dropped it over the side and eased it to the bottom. I felt the weight hit bottom at sixty-three feet. "We could have just used the anchor line, but I want you to see how this works."

Then I pulled out two Jon Lines. I explained to her what they were for. "On accent, we can hook the carabiner to the downline and stay at a certain depth while we decompress. This relieves the strain of trying to hold on to the downline, especially in a strong current. We really won't need it, but I want you to use it at thirty feet as we come up."

Stacy listened and examined the Jon Line carefully. She hooked it to her belt. Then she hooked a small box to her belt.

"What's that?" I asked.

"An underwater camera. I bought it yesterday."

"You should get some good pictures."

"And videos."

We sat on the swim platform and then slid into the water. We started a slow descent.

I watched her carefully as we moved toward the bottom. She was doing everything right.

We had two tanks each. We would dive Joe's Tug for a while and then return to the boat. Then we would go do some reef diving.

We swam to Joe's Tug. It's surprising to see it for the first time, especially if you're expecting a tug boat. The shrimp boat was torn apart by a hurricane after it was dropped there. There was a thirty-foot gap between the bow and the mid-body of the wreckage.

The fish were thick around the boat. They created a rainbow of color. Stacy looked at me and gave me a thumbs up then took her camera off her belt and started snapping pictures.

We circled the bow and peeked inside, then moved to the main body. Debris was scattered everywhere.

Suddenly Stacy swam to me and got behind me. She pointed to the left. I looked over to see a giant scalloped hammerhead shark swimming past. I gave her a thumbs up and pulled her back around me. I pointed to my eyes and then back at the shark. I didn't want her to miss this. She was lucky to see one on her first dive. She took some pictures of it.

The shark swam in a circle around the boat and then moved on until it was out of sight.

We explored the surrounding area for another half-hour taking movies of each other before I pointed to the surface. She nodded and we swam to the downline. Holding on to it, we ascended slowly to thirty feet. She watched her gauge and stopped. She hooked onto the Jon Line. We held the line and waited a few minutes then moved toward the surface.

At the boat, I removed my tank and pushed it onto the swim platform then took Stacy's. We climbed aboard met by two enthusiastic dogs who proceeded to lick us to death.

"God, that was fantastic," Stacy said, pushing Hank away from her face. "I've never seen anything so beautiful."

"It's a different world down there," I said.

"That shark, wow. What was it?"

"Hammerhead."

"Are they dangerous?"

"They certainly can be. They mostly feed off fish, stingrays, and smaller sharks. But if some idiot baits the water, as some do, they'll go into a feeding frenzy and eat anything they can catch, and they are very fast."

"Are we going back down?"

'We're going to a reef off the coast. You'll love it."

"Let's eat something and catch our breath first."

Stan and Holly sat in the boat and ate breakfast. They were anchored about fifty feet off the shore from the Sunset Grill. A few people were sitting at tables along the water's edge eating. One man stood and yelled toward them, "Cam." He waved.

Stan waved back vigorously then Holly waved. The man motioned for them to come to shore. Stan waved again, pointed out to the bay, and started the engine. They idled away slowly.

"That was perfect," Holly said. "Someone who knows Cam took you for him. Now he's been seen in the area."

Stan cruised around Boot Key into the mouth of Sister Creek and skidded the boat onto the sand of Sombrero Beach.

"Here we are," he said. Looking at his watch he said, "Forty-five minutes. I'm going to walk the beach. You stay here."

"I'll call you if I see anything," she said.

Stan jumped onto the beach and walked toward the park area. There were picnic tables and a volleyball court, two buildings that held the restrooms and a gazebo.

A few people were already there setting up camp in the few shaded areas. Stan walked down to the beach and along the water back to the boat.

"This should work fine," he said. "There isn't a lot of cover. I think I can surprise them in the open."

He reached into a bag and pulled out two nine-millimeter Glocks. He put them into the waistband of his shorts and pulled his shirt down over them.

Holly raised the front cushion and pulled out her AR-15 rifle. "I'll be ready if you need me," she said.

Stan smiled and kissed her. "You're always ready when I need you."

"Don't forget, you said we will have sex when this is over."

"I've been thinking about it ever since I said it. I'll see you in a few."

He picked up his ball cap and a book, stepped out of the boat again, and walked to a picnic table on the edge of the park. He sat and pulled his ball cap down to partially block his face and opened the book.

Holly backed the boat away from the beach on the creek side and idled into the Straits a hundred yards from the beach.

Chapter 9

John Bexley sat in his car facing Sombrero Beach. He arrived early as he usually did for a meeting. For this one it was even more important to be there early. He wanted to see how many guards Rafael would bring and hide around the beach. He was glad he hadn't come alone. Holly was going to protect him from out on the water.

He stepped out of his car and used his binoculars to scan the beach and the water. Then he saw her. Holly was floating about a hundred yards off the beach. She was wearing a blonde wig and scanning the beach with her binoculars. When she turned toward John, he waved. She waved back. Good, they were in position and ready.

Holly called Stan and gave him John's location.

We ate our power bars and drank some electrolytes. "I prefer the chocolate honeybuns," I said.

"You can't live off those things, Cam."

"I can try. If you dunk them in Wild Turkey, they take on a whole new flavor."

"I'm limiting you to two Wild Turkeys a day. I want you in good health. You're too much fun to waste away. From now on you run with me in the mornings and eat healthily."

"I would never have brought you out here if I'd known you were going to try to ruin my life."

"You'll thank me someday."

"Well, I don't know about that."

"You will. Are you ready for another dive?"

"Sure. Grab the new tank and get it ready. We'll be there in twenty minutes," I said as I pulled in the anchor and downline.

I dropped anchor again just outside the reef I had chosen for her. "We'll use the anchor line this time instead of the downline," I told her.

"Two other boats were anchored within a hundred yards. One of them belonged to Donny Perkins. I hadn't seen him for about a month. I thought he went back to Alaska for the summer.

We slipped into the water again. I stayed back and watched everything she did. I couldn't help being proud of her. When she'd first told me she wanted to dive, I had thought she might be a little too much of an airhead to get it right. Now I felt bad about that. She'd turned out to be a great diver and I'd learned over the last month that she was quite intelligent also. During our long talks on the boat, while she was watching over me, I found out she has a master's degree in business. Since she works at Coyote Ugly, I figured she was doing what she could to make ends meet. But she comes from a wealthy family and could have any life she chooses. This is the life she has chosen. She loves being wild and free. It suits her well.

Bexley saw a black SUV pull into the parking lot. It sat and idled for a minute before it pulled into a parking spot. The meeting was still fifteen minutes from now.

He kept an eye on the car and waited. Finally, a Cuban man got out of the passenger side and stood in front of the car looking up and down the beach. Rafael Camacho. The driver must have been Mario Santana. With the dark windows, it was impossible to see inside the car. There could be two more in the back seat. As if he sensed John's disinclination to come forward, Rafael walked to the rear door and opened it, then moved away. John could see inside now. It was empty. Then his phone rang.

"Yea?" he said.

"They dropped two men out a block back," Holly said. "They're entering the park from the west end now."

John hung up and watched the west end. Two men who didn't look like they belonged were entering the park together. They split up and moved toward the east where the meeting was to take place. *Backup. That's okay and smart.*

Bexley got out of his car, opened his rear door, took out a small bag, and walked to the third picnic table. He stopped and looked at Rafael, gave him a nod, and then went toward him.

John sat at the table. Rafael sat across from him. John looked at Mario and waved him to come and join them. He did.

When they were all settled, they started their business talk. John slid the bag across the table to Mario and told him to go back to the car and test it. Mario stood and left.

Stan watched all this over the book he was reading two tables away. He would wait until Mario returned before he would approach them.

He took the time to survey the beach. Not a large crowd but maybe fifteen people. That didn't count the two Holly called and told him about after she had called John. He'd have to make his escape quickly and hope Holly was accurate with her rifle.

Five minutes later, Mario returned to the table. Rafael looked up at him and Mario nodded. *I guess the coke passed the test.*

Stan removed his hat. That was the signal to Holly to get ready. Twenty seconds later, Stan stood and walked toward the table. He stopped and called, "Bexley!"

John turned to look. The sun was behind Stan. He shaded his eyes a second; then they widened. "Cam!"

"That's right. Now it's your time to die."

Stan pulled his gun from his waistband and opened fire. John dove for the ground behind the table while Mario and Rafael pulled their guns and returned fire. Stan moved his aim and shot Mario in the chest. At the same time, he saw Rafael's head explode. Holly.

Now John had his gun out and was firing back at Stan who dove behind another table. They each fired in rapid succession. Then Stan felt a bullet tear at his shirt. But it was coming from behind him. He turned to take a quick look just as a man with his gun raised flew off his feet and hit the ground. Holly again, but there was still one behind him somewhere.

The patrons of the beach were running in all directions. Stan saw one man hit the ground hard and stay down. *He's been hit.*

He couldn't do anything about the one behind him, so he turned his attention back to John.

"Cam, I'm glad you're here. It'll save me a trip to Key West," John yelled.

Stan fired again. Then he heard a bullet ricochet off his table. He turned again and saw the other shooter hiding behind the restroom. He wasn't going to be able to get to him. Now Stan had no choice but to get out of Dodge. He called Holly.

"Cover me. I'm coming to the boat."

"I'll spin it around at the beach."

Stan put his phone in his pocket and yelled, "Stacy! Turn the boat around!"

Holly put her gun on automatic and pushed the throttle forward. With one hand on the wheel and one on the gun, she opened fire in short, accurate bursts.

Stan stood and ran for the boat. Just as he reached it, he felt a tug at his shoulder. He'd been hit. He dove into the boat, grabbed Holly's gun, and turned to open fire again.

He saw two more civilians hit the ground. More collateral damage.

Holly pushed the throttles forward again and they sped away. "Are you okay?" she called.

"Yeah, just a nick. Fuck, I didn't get Bexley."

"What do you wanna do?"

"Turn north and try to beat him to the highway. I might be able to see him and get a shot off."

Holly turned hard and skimmed the waves toward the Overseas Highway. They could see John speeding parallel to them on Sombrero Road. He was moving fast.

"Shit," Stan said. "Get closer to the bank."

She did, having to whip the boat out occasionally to avoid hitting a dock.

Stan leaned on the windshield to steady his hand and fired another blast toward the car. He missed. "Keep going," he said, waving her forward.

Bexley was pulling away from them now. Then they saw two police cars pass John heading for the beach. Holly pulled the throttle back and spun the boat around. "We can't get caught in this canal," she said. "We have to get out of here."

"But Bexley's going to get away."

"Maybe, but who is he going to go after?"

Stan cleared his head. "Yeah, Cam Derringer."

"I'm heading to Joe's Tug," Holly said. "When we get there, maybe they'll still be underwater. We can stash the clothes on their boat."

Stan took Cam's clothes off and slipped on his own clothes then took the wheel while Holly did the same. Then he gave the controls back to her.

How many civs did you take out?" Stan asked.

"I think I hit four."

"Good. That'll make sure they investigate. If it was just cartel they wouldn't try too hard."

"We're almost there. If they're in the boat, we'll visit them tonight and hide the clothes in the boat then."

The closer they got to Joe's Tug the more Stan could tell the GPS was off. "They're not at the tug," he said. "Turn forty degrees starboard."

They followed the signal until they saw the boat anchored offshore about a mile. Stan's friend, Lance Peters, was sitting in his boat about a quarter mile from Cam's. Holly pulled up to it.

"Are they diving?" Stan asked.

"Yep, been down about fifteen minutes," Lance said.

"Did anyone see them at Joe's Tug?"

"Nope, I didn't let anyone near them."

"Okay, thanks. You can go now."

Lance started his boat and sped away.

Chapter 10

We were still exploring the reef when I saw a shadow from another boat overhead. It stopped about ten feet from our boat and then drifted toward it. I motioned to Stacy that I was going topside and would be back. She looked up and saw the other boat too. She motioned that she would go with me. I shook my head no.

Pirates are known to invade boats where the divers are down. There was nothing in our boat to steal and I knew Walter wouldn't allow anyone to come aboard while we were down there.

"Damn, there are two dogs on board," Stan said as they drifted toward Cam's boat.

The big Golden Retriever started to bark and was aggressive. The chocolate lab followed suit and barked too.

"That's Cam's Retriever. He's not going to let us get on that boat. Let's go. We'll take care of it tonight."

Holly turned the boat and they sped away. "This was a total disaster. Nothing went right," Holly said.

"It wasn't your normal kill-and-leave hit. There were too many side jobs that needed to be done."

"Okay, it'll take us a little longer, but it will be done."

I surfaced and looked around. The boat was gone, but the dogs were still barking. I looked to the west and saw a boat heading toward Key West.

I climbed on board and calmed the dogs.

"Good boys," I said and petted them.

I watched for a minute to make sure they weren't going to return then slid back into the water. Stacy was waiting for me at the thirty-foot marker. I gave her the thumbs up and we descended to the reef again.

While we were down I signaled for Stacy to take her mouthpiece out. She did. Then I gave her mine. She blew it clear and placed it in her mouth. We switched back and forth a few times. I nodded to her and she put hers back in her mouth. Well done.

A few minutes later, she checked her gauge and motioned for me to return to the surface. She was right. We were running out of air. I wanted her to be the one to realize it.

Back in the boat, she was elated once more. We stripped out of our dive gear and high-fived each other. She threw her arms around me and kissed me. "I will never, ever forget you and what you have done for me," she said.

"Likewise," I said.

She hugged the dogs and told them all about what was down there. They pretended to be listening.

"We need to celebrate," she said.

I opened the cooler and pulled out a bottle of Wild Turkey and two glasses.

"Cheers," I said as I handed her a glass. "Say when," and I poured.

I quit before she said when.

"Enough," I said. "You'll be snockered."

I poured myself one and we clanked our glasses together. "To new memories and old friends. Never lose either," I said.

We sat in the boat and sipped our drinks. Stacy pulled out some cheese and crackers from her bag. We were sitting on the bow cushion with the dogs at our feet waiting for us to drop a crumb. Stacy leaned toward me. I put my arm on the top of the cushion and she rested her head on my chest.

"I could live out here on the water forever," she said.

"You do live on the water. Have you ever taken your boat out?"

"No, I wouldn't know how to operate it."

"You mean no one ever showed you how to captain a boat?"

She looked up at me and raised her eyebrows. "Not yet."

"You want me to take you out on it? I can teach you. If you pick up on it as fast as you did this, it'll be a breeze."

"We'll see. You know Diane and Jack will be back next week. Then Kailey will be here soon and I'll lose you again. This is fun having you all to myself."

"I'll find the time to teach you. Don't worry about that."

"Promise?"

"Promise."

We gave the dogs each a cracker. It didn't seem to satisfy them. Stacy pulled a bag of rawhide treats out. That got their attention. She gave them each a few and they moved to opposite sides of the boat to chew on them.

"Ready?" I finally asked.

"Not really but I guess we'd better go in."

I pulled the anchor up and stowed it. Stacy moved back beside me and the dogs took their place on the bow. The water was smooth with just a slight two-foot rolling wave occasionally.

We pulled into Blue Harbor Point around noon. Stacy stepped off the boat and tied it off. I handed her the gear and told her I would stash it on my boat until tomorrow when I'd refill the tanks.

"You wanna go get a bite to eat?" I asked.

"I'd love to."

We let the dogs do their thing then put them inside. Walter didn't protest. He headed straight for the sofa and crashed in the air conditioning.

"I know how you feel, old boy."

I showered, dressed, and went to Stacy's boat. She was ready and sitting on her lanai.

"Shall we?" I said.

"Where to?"

"How about Bistro 245?"

"You buying?"

"Hmm, maybe we should just go to McDonald's."

"Too late; you've got my tastebuds perked now."

"Alright, let's go."

We were eating at an outside table when Ryan Chase, Stacy's sometime boyfriend and sheriff's deputy, walked past.

"Ryan!" I called.

He turned. When he saw us, he smiled and came to the table.

Stacy stood and kissed him. "Join us? Cam's buying."

Ryan laughed and pulled out a chair. The waiter came to the table and Ryan ordered a beer.

"I wish Stacy was as cheap a date as you are," I said. "She ordered half the menu."

"She's an eater," he said.

"We've been diving," she said and told him all about it.

"That's great," he said. "I guess you haven't heard about the mess at Sombrero Beach then."

"No, we were kinda out of touch today," I said. "What happened?"

"There were three guys on the beach having some kind of meeting. A man came in guns blazing and took out two of them. Then two more men started firing from behind him. They were killed by a woman on a boat waiting for the first shooter. The other two got away. One they found dead on the beach was a three-and-out wiseguy from the Santana cartel. Four civilians were hit. Three are dead."

I froze for a moment. The Santana cartel was who Malinda said she thought John Bexley was meeting with. Could it be he was involved in all this?

"Do you have any ID on the ones that got away?"

"Not yet. We're going to get the beach cams. Hopefully, they caught something. I do have a little note for ya though. One of the witnesses said she thought she heard one of the guys call the shooter Cam. You weren't there were you?"

"If I was there they'd all be dead," I said.

"I believe it."

"It's too bad what happened. With the cartels involved, we'll never find who did it. But we're gonna give it a go. If it was just the cartels shooting each other up, we wouldn't go to the trouble, but three civilians who were enjoying a day at the beach are dead now."

"Good luck with it," I said, but I knew I was going to go investigate myself. Bexley had to be involved with this. It was time to bring him down.

"Thanks for the beer," Ryan said, "but I have to go. Are you free tonight?" he asked Stacy.

She looked at me.

"You're free," I said.

"Yeah, what do ya wanna do?"

"How about supper and some wine on the beach?"

"Okay."

He stood, fist-bumped me, and told me thanks for the beer again.

Chapter 11

I said goodbye to Stacy at her boat and walked the dock to mine. When I opened the door, Walter was lying on his back with all four legs straight up in the air. Was he playing dead?

"Walter, what's up?"

He fell over sideways and opened his eyes.

"Are you dead?" I said in dog talk. It's like baby talk but you try not to say it in front of anyone.

He didn't move his body but his tail was going to town on the floor. I bent down and rubbed his head as I passed him. He jumped up and followed me to the bathroom. I closed the door in his face. When I came out, he was sitting up and staring at the door.

"You are weirder all the time," I said.

He fell over on his back and stuck his legs back up.

My cell phone rang. The ID showed it was Malinda. No doubt this was going to be about Sombrero.

"What's up?" I answered.

"Cam, tell me you didn't go to Sombrero Beach today."

"I didn't go to Sombrero Beach today."

"Did you hear what happened?"

"Yep, Ryan told me."

"Have you seen the beach cam tapes?"

"Nope, I just found out. I was out diving with Stacy all day."

"Get those tapes and take a look. Then I want you to call me. We have some talking to do."

"I tell you, I wasn't there. And how am I going to get the tapes?"

"We had a CIA agent watching Bexley since he arrived. He saw the gunfight but couldn't get to them in time. When he checked Mario's body, he found a recorder. He had been recording the meeting. Agent Eric Townsend has the recording and the film from the beach cams. He said when you put the two together, it looks like you and Stacy were the ones who pulled it off."

"We were diving," I said.

"Get the tapes and stay out of sight. He said he'd meet you in the Sea Turtle Hospital parking lot. Here's his phone number."

She gave me the number and I wrote it down.

"You might be in big trouble."

"How could I be in trouble?"

"Call me," she said and hung up.

What the hell? What was she talking about? I grabbed my keys and headed out the door. Walter came to my side. I thought about it. "You wanna go to Marathon?"

On the drive there my phone rang again. The caller ID showed "Curt." It was Curt James, a friend whose father lives one block from Sombrero Beach.

"Hey Curt, what's up?"

"Are you okay, Cam?"

"Yeah, why?"

"Because of what happened here at the beach. A friend just showed us his cellphone movie of the shoot-out. He thought I'd like to see it before he turned it over to the police. He knew you and I are friends."

"And?"

"And I talked him into putting it off for a few hours."

"Why?"

"Because it shows you and Stacy."

"Curt, I don't know what you're talking about, but I'm on my way there now. Brittany told me to go to Marathon and meet a guy about the tapes. I'll come to your house afterward. I'll see you in a half-hour."

I pulled into the parking lot at the hospital. As soon as I did a man got out of a black SUV and came to my passenger door. I unlocked it and he climbed in.

"Look at these, Cam," he said, flipping his laptop on. The scene at the beach was peaceful. Then he switched on a recorder on his phone. The voice came in clear. They were talking about a drug deal then someone called Bexley. He said, "Cam." More talking and gunfire started.

The shooter looked a lot like me, but the beach cams were not all that clear. At the end of the fight, the man they called Cam turned to the boat and called for Stacy.

What the hell? This didn't make any sense.

"I showed this to Brittany," he said. "She said it did look a lot like you."

"I was diving with a friend in Key West. I wasn't there."

"That's what she said. I believe her, but someone is messing with you bad. We're going to keep these tapes and hope no others turn up."

"Too late," I said. "A friend called me and said he saw another one from a cell phone. It shows the same thing you have here."

"Shit. Does he have it?"

"He does, he's going to give it to me, but I'm sure it's not the only copy."

"I'll report everything to Brittany. She's going to handle it," he said.

I left him and drove to Curt and John James' house.

When I passed the beach, there were four police cars and three sheriff cars sitting on the street with the blue lights flashing. Crime tape surrounded the beach.

I turned right onto John's street and entered their driveway. The gate opened and I pulled in. I saw the gate close behind me.

Rose, John's wife, greeted Walter and me halfway up the walk. She's a beautiful red-haired girl John married about five years ago, a few years after his divorce.

"Come on in before someone sees you," she said after hugging me and petting Walter.

I still had no idea what this was all about, but I was getting a feeling it wasn't going to be good for me.

Curt and John were waiting inside. We shook hands and took a seat on the sofa. Walter sat at my feet.

"Would you like anything to drink?" Rose asked.

"I'm not sure. What's going on?"

They all exchanged glances.

"Here," Curt said as he handed me a cell phone. "Press the play button."

I took the phone but kept looking at the three of them.

"Play it," Rose said.

I turned my attention to the phone. Someone was filming a peaceful day at the beach. Then a man stood and started to walk toward the camera. Not directly but at an angle.

The volume was on and turned up. The man in the film was the one I saw before and he looked a lot like me. If I didn't know any better, I'd have said it *was* me.

"Bexley," the man called.

The camera swung slightly to the left as another man stood. It was John Bexley.

"Cam," he said.

"Now it's your turn to die," the first man said as he pulled out two guns and started firing.

The camera person dropped down behind a table but kept filming. The carnage that followed was sickening.

I looked closely at the man who looked like me. I recognized the clothes he was wearing. They were mine. The Rum City Bar T-shirt he had on had a tear at the neck in front where I'd had cut it to let more air in.

Then the camera swung to the water. A woman was standing in a boat aiming a rifle toward the crowd. She fired and a man behind the first shooter fell to the ground.

The boat and the woman looked familiar too. This was all too strange. It was Stacy and me shooting up the beach.

Then the shooter called to the boat, "Stacy, turn the boat around!"

The scene went on until the man ran to the boat, jumped in, and the boat left. When it took off, the camera zoomed in on the stern. The words *Diane's Days* stood out.

"What the hell?" I said.

I handed the phone back to Curt.

"I'm going to ask you one time," John said. "Were you and Stacy there this morning?"

"No. We were diving all morning at Joe's Tug. Call and ask her."

"She wouldn't be the most credible alibi. Did anyone else see you out there?"

"I don't think so. How did someone film us at the beach when we weren't there? It doesn't make any sense."

"No, it doesn't. As a matter of fact, it's impossible. The police are going to get the beach cams or someone else is going to turn in a phone like this one. And they'll be looking for you."

"The beach cams are already taken care of. The CIA has them. One of the agents showed it to me. It wasn't as clear as this one, but it was damning enough."

"Shit, Cam," John said.

"Do you believe it was us?"

"I did until you told me it wasn't. Now we have to find out who it was and clear this thing up."

"Why would someone go to all this trouble to kill these cartel members and try to make it look like I did it?"

"Did you know any of them?"

"Yes. The guy who stood and called him Cam is John Bexley, the one who shot me a few months ago."

They exchanged glances again.

"Yeah, I know," I said. "It makes it look like a revenge shooting. I swear it wasn't me."

"I want you to stay here tonight," Curt said. "I'm going down to the beach now. I know most of the local police and the sheriff's department. I'll see what I can find out."

"Do they know that you know me?"

"Mike Owens does. He's with the sheriff's department."

"Yeah, I remember him. We went fishing one day."

"I'll talk to him first if he's there. He'd be the only one who would recognize you. I doubt if they have any film yet."

"It won't take the others long once they see it. My picture shows up on the news quite often."

"I'll go with you," John said. "I've got a lot of pull here. I'll try to get this stopped before it gets started."

Curt and John left on foot and walked to the beach.

"Would you like that drink now?" Rose asked.

"Yeah, I think so."

Then I thought about Stacy. I needed to call her and tell her what was going on. She could be in big trouble once the news came out.

"Here ya go," Rose said as she returned to the room. "Wild Turkey."

"Thanks."

I took a strong hit off the drink and then stood.

"I can't just sit here," I said. "I have to get to work on this. It looks like Bexley got away. He'll be looking for me. He thinks it was me who shot at him."

"At least wait until they get back. Nothing is going to happen in the next fifteen minutes," Rose said.

I paced the floor worrying about what could happen. Walter paced with me.

"I need to call Stacy," I said.

"Wait, Cam. Let's see what they find out; then you can tell her everything."

John and Curt stopped at the crime tape and scanned the area. "There's Mike," Curt said, pointing to an officer who was digging a bullet out of a picnic table.

They waited for Mike to look their way before signaling to him. He waved and came to where they were standing outside the tape.

"Hey John, Curt," he said as he neared them.

"What do you have?" John asked.

"Not much. The beach cam tapes are blank and we can't find anyone who filmed any of the shooting. The only thing we have to go on is one witness who said she heard one of the guys call out, 'Cam.' Then she heard someone call, 'Stacy.' That's not much. As a matter of fact, the only Cam I know is Derringer and I know he wouldn't do this."

"No, he wouldn't," Curt said.

"How many dead?" John asked.

"Three mob guys and three civilians who were in the wrong place at the wrong time."

"That's too bad about the civs," Curt said.

"The witness said it was like an afterthought. They were in the boat leaving when the woman turned her automatic on the crowd."

"Who would do that?" John said disgustedly.

"Who indeed. We'll find them and they'll pay."

"Who's leading the case?"

"Roberts, right now. A lieutenant from MPD."

"Yeah, I know 'im," John said. "Why do you say right now?"

"Miami Cartel. More than likely the CIA will be here shortly. They have people to protect."

"You mean cartel members?"

"Yeah."

"Fuck 'im," Curt said angrily. "If I find 'em and they're guilty, they'll pay."

"I feel the same way, Curt, but we can't fly off the handle. You let us take care of things."

John put his hand on Curt's arm to calm him.

"If you learn anything, will ya let us know?" John said.

"You've got it."

"Thanks."

They returned to the house where Rose was trying to calm Cam down.

"It's okay, Cam," Curt said. "They don't have any film of the attack. Right now it seems this is the only one."

"Right now, yes," I said, "but what about the ones that start showing up when people realize what they have?"

"We'll handle that when the time comes."

"What do they have now?"

"They have the names Cam and Stacy."

"Great."

"Did anyone see the two of you diving?" John asked.

"Not that I know of. It was just the two of us out there, along with Walter and Hank. Someone was doing some testing in the area and they locked it down except for us.

"You took the dogs with you?"

"Yeah, Stacy wanted them along."

"There was no mention of any dogs at the beach."

"I don't think that's going to make a good alibi."

"No, probably not, but it does create a little doubt."

"I think I should go back to Key West. I'm afraid Bexley will show up there to find me. Stacy's there alone. He might take it out on her."

"Okay, Cam, I think you're right. Keep in contact and we'll let you know what we can find out. I'm going to send the movie to your phone and delete this one."

"Your friend will be pissed."

"He'll be paid for it."

"Send me the bill."

I went to the door where Walter was already waiting. "Thanks, guys, for the help," I said as I opened the door.

"We'll get this figured out. Don't worry," Rose said and hugged me.

The gate opened and I drove out. When I turned at the end of the street, I was staring right at the beach. The police were still investigating the scene. Now the crowd of onlookers had grown.

I cruised by slowly and then sped up when I got away from the area. I turned south on the Overseas Highway and sped up more. I wanted to get to Stacy before Bexley could. The man was capable of anything.

My car started flashing blue. Then I realized the blue lights were from the police car behind me.

Chapter 12

"License and registration, please," the officer said as I slid the window down.

He was standing behind the door with his hand on his gun.

"What's the problem, officer?" I asked.

"You were doing fifty-eight in a thirty-five," he said and held out his hand. "License and registration."

I handed him the documents.

"What were you doing in Marathon today?"

"Just visiting a friend."

"Who might that be?"

Why did he want to know all this? Just give me the damn ticket and let's get on our way.

I said, "John James," before I thought. I didn't want to get him involved.

He looked at my driver's license. "Cam Derringer?"

"Yes sir."

"I know that name. You're a PI from Key West."

"That's right."

"You helped us on a case a few years ago. My partner still talks about how you saved his life."

He handed me the papers back. "Slow down, Cam. I'll tell John he owes me one."

"Thank you. I don't usually drive like that."

He went back to his car and pulled back out on the highway. A thought came to my mind. *Now they have a record of me being in Marathon.*

It was late when I returned to Key West. Stacy would already be gone with Ryan on their date. At least she'd be in good hands.

When I pulled into the parking lot, I noticed Ryan's car was there. Maybe they decided to eat in.

They were sitting on the lanai. Walter ran to her for a pet and hopefully a treat. He got both.

"Hi guys," I said.

"Hey, Cam," Stacy said. "Where ya been?"

"Just out and about."

"We're having a drink before we go to supper," Ryan said. "Want one?"

"No, thanks. I think I'll turn in for the night."

"Too much activity today?" Stacy asked.

"You could say that."

I turned to leave then stopped. "You two be safe tonight," I said. "Whoever shot up the beach is out there somewhere and I don't trust 'im."

"What makes you think they'd come here?" Ryan asked.

"I don't know if they would, but just be careful."

"Yeah, okay, Cam," Stacy said more seriously and gave me a look of concern.

Walter and I went to the boat. I fed him again and found his water bowl in the bottom drawer of my dresser. That was the second time he'd hidden it there and I had no idea how.

A minute later, Stacy said from behind me, "What's up, Cam?"

I turned to see her standing inside the parlor door.

"Where's Ryan?" I asked, looking behind her.

"I told him I wanted to talk to you alone for a minute."

"Good. Come in and sit down."

"This sounds serious."

"It is."

She got a frightened look on her face and moved to the sofa.

I handed her my phone and told her to push play. She watched, glancing at me once in a while, wide-eyed.

When it was over, she handed the phone back to me but didn't say anything. I could tell she was in a mild state of shock.

"Someone really set us up. The man at the picnic table is John Bexley."

"The guy who shot you?"

"Yes, and he got away. I'm afraid he'll come here looking for us."

"Us?"

I nodded my head slowly letting it sink in.

"He thinks it was me trying to kill 'im and more than likely that it was you in the boat."

"The boat is even an exact copy. And, those were my clothes, and yours."

"Yep, someone went to great detail to set us up. You can't tell Ryan about this. The police haven't seen this. The only ones who know are John, Curt, and Rose, plus the guy who took it. And the CIA."

"The CIA? What are we going to do?"

"You're going to go away. I'm going to find Bexley and finish this."

"I'm not going to leave you to clean this up by yourself. I can shoot. You taught me how last year."

"I know, but it will be easier if I'm not worried about you."

"What am I going to tell Ryan?"

"You'll be safe with him tonight. Don't say anything about this. I'll see you when you get home."

"I don't know if I can go with him now. He'll know something's up."

"Just go eat then tell him you're not feeling well. When you get home, call me."

Stacy stood and hugged me. "I'm scared," she said. I saw a tear run down her face.

I put my arms around her and held her. This was the last thing I wanted. I decided to return to her boat with her to fill Ryan in on a little of what was going on. It was risky to tell anyone, but I trust him.

"What's the problem?" he asked as we approached the boat. "Are you okay, Stacy?"

She nodded and looked at me. We sat at the table with him.

"The shoot-out at the beach today," I said. "One of the guys is John Bexley."

"The guy who shot you. How do you know this?"

"A friend who was there recognized him. Anyway, I'm afraid he'll come here looking for me now."

"Why? He's had two months to come for you. He knows where you live."

"He might think I'm the one who tried to kill him today. That's all I can tell you. Don't ask any more questions."

"But what about Stacy?"

"She might be in danger just by being my friend."

Ryan thought about that for a few seconds.

"I know there's a lot more to it than you're telling me, but for now, good enough. I'll keep an eye on Stacy and you do what you need to do. I suppose you want me to keep this between us."

"Thanks, Ryan. I'll fill you in on more when I can."

"Stacy can stay at my house tonight. Do you have anywhere you can go?"

"I'll stay at Diane's house. She won't be back until late tomorrow night."

"Good," Ryan said and stood. He looked at Stacy. "Get some clothes together."

"Don't I have any say in this?" she asked.

"It's for the best," I said. "I'll call you tomorrow."

She looked at both of us then stood and disappeared inside. Her world has been rocked and I was going to do something about it. This was another one of those times when I'd gotten her in trouble and she expected me to get her out. I would do my best to protect her.

After they left for Ryan's house, I went over my options. I could put myself out there and hope Bexley missed with his first shot, or I could hide in the dark and wait for him to come to me. The only thing was he might go for Stacy before he came for me.

I could go to the police and have them put out an APB on Bexley. But there would be a lot of questions to answer. Answers I didn't have yet.

No, I was in a hell of a mess this time. No one was there with me. I usually have a team around me. Jack and three very strong women.

My cell rang. "Hey, Malinda."

"You didn't call me back. I'm worried."

"Yeah, me too. Did you see the film?"

"Yes, from the beach cam. Where did you see them?"

"A friend of Curt James had one on his phone. He gave it to Curt when he saw I was on it."

"How do you explain it, Cam?"

"I can't and do I have to?"

She hesitated. "The boat said *Diane's Days* on the back."

"Yeah, I saw that too. Also, the shooter yelled for Stacy to turn the boat around and Bexley called him Cam. If it was me, would I be that stupid?"

"If it was you, you are that stupid."

"Okay, okay, it wasn't me or Stacy, but someone sure nailed me."

"I've been doing a little investigation on my end. It seems Camata has gotten in touch with an assassin known as Stan Whittle. He's tall and looks a lot like you. With a little make-up and copying your mannerisms, he could pass as you."

"Why now? Why would he do that?"

"He's probably still pissed that you shot 'im. I know I would be. He's trying to get you killed or put away without me knowing it was him. Too late. He's a dead man. I warned him."

"Won't that put Bexley in charge of the cartel on his own?"

"Bexley was supposed to get killed. Stan fucked it up."

"Well, that still doesn't help me any. More than likely Bexley is down here looking for me and Stacy. I've got her hidden, but I'm going after Bexley before he can find her."

"Don't do that, he's dangerous. I'll send help to find him."

"I'm dangerous too, if you haven't noticed, and I can't wait. I'll talk to you later," I said and hung up.

This wasn't going to be good. There were too many scenarios for how it could turn out. One was that Bexley had returned to Bermuda and might come here in a few months to get me. I'd never know when he showed up.

John Bexley called Camata on his private number. It rang four times before he answered. John knew he kept his phone on his belt. He was trying to decide whether to answer or not.

"John," Camata answered. "How did it go?"

"Holly teamed up with Cam Derringer and tried to kill me. That's how it went. What the fuck?"

"I can't believe Holly would do that."

"She did. She shot at me and also took out one of the Santana Cartel guys. Then she helped Cam escape."

"I'll take care of her. You just come on back here."

"Fuck you! I'm going to find Cam and kill that son of a bitch. Then I'm going to kill Holly. He called her Stacy. I don't know what that was all about, but they screwed up big time. Holly was supposed to be backing me up."

"Whatever it takes. Just be sure to get Cam. He's been a pain in our side."

"Oh, I will. I'll get them all," Bexley said and hung up.

Camata smiled to himself. *If he manages to kill Cam, that's great. If Cam kills him, that's good too. If Holly and Stan get killed, I'll save a lot of money. I don't see any way I can come out on the bottom of this deal.*

Chapter 13

Malinda called Kailey in Manila.

"Yes," she answered.

"We're good," Malinda said, meaning the phone was secure.

"Hey girl, what's up?"

"Cam."

"What's he done now?"

Malinda went through the whole story not leaving out any details.

"I can be there in two days," Kailey said.

"You have to finish your assignment there first. It's important. I'll take care of this. I just wanted to let you know."

"Hang on a minute," Kailey said.

Fifteen seconds later, Malinda heard a pop from a silenced rifle. A sound she'd heard many times before.

Kailey came back on the phone. "I'm finished here. I'll be in Key West in two days."

"Roger that. I'll see you there."

I sat on the deck of Jack's boat at Garrison Bight with Walter. We were drinking a Wild Turkey. It was supposed to be mine, but I mistakenly set it down for a minute. When I looked at Walter, he was lickin' his chops. I picked up the drink to take a swallow, but it was empty.

"You're a lush," I said. He burped.

I needed a plan of action. How was I going to find a man who was hunting for me? The easiest and dumbest way would be to make myself visible. That wouldn't be too hard. Murder Fest Key West was starting the next day. They'd asked me to be a guest speaker. Something to give the authors a little inspiration. I had been working on a speech. It included some of the gory details of the Fest two years ago when I helped solve a case involving a serial killer during their meetings.

It would draw a lot of publicity and be on the news. I called Henry Tally, their chairman, and told him I would be there.

"That's great, Cam. Can you make it at eleven?"

"Sure, that should be fine."

"Okay, don't leave out any details."

"I won't. Will there be any security there? You know, after the last time I'd think you'd want some."

"We have a security team in place. We like to write about murders, but we definitely don't want any."

"Good," I said.

"Are you expecting trouble?"

"You never know."

"No, you don't."

"See ya tomorrow at eleven."

"Come early for appetizers and drinks if you want."

"I'll be there."

After we hung up, I rewrote my speech. The story I was going to deliver would knock their socks off.

We left the boat around ten thirty and drove to Diane's house. The refrigerator was close to empty, but I managed to scrape up a snack of cheese and crackers, pickles, and a can of mixed fruit.

She kept treats and dog food there for Walter. He wolfed it down. I took my time and enjoyed my snack along with a glass of wine.

I wasn't worried that Bexley would attack me that night. He didn't know of Diane's house. As far as the docks went, Stacy wasn't there, my boat was empty, and everyone else was gone.

We were sitting in the backyard in front of her fountain when Walter jumped up and started barking.

I sprang to my feet and reached for the gun I keep in my belt. It wasn't there. I'd left it on the kitchen table.

Walter ran to the gate by the driveway, still barking. I ran toward the house and then moved along the bushes to where Walter was still barking.

I looked around the corner in time to see a figure in the dark running away from the house. I couldn't tell if it was Bexley, but it was a big man like him.

I opened the gate and ran down the driveway. Walter passed me and turned the corner in front of the house next door. When I came around the house, Walter was gone and so was the man.

I heard a yell in the distance and could hear Walter growling and barking. It sounded as if he had caught whoever was there.

When I was three houses down, I saw a figure on the ground under Walter, who wasn't going to let him get away.

"Call this dog off me," the guy said.

"Walter!" I yelled.

He backed up a step but didn't turn his attention away.

I grabbed a hold of the man and pulled him up, bending his arm behind him. It wasn't Bexley.

"What are you doing out here?" I asked, still forcing his arm.

"Nothing, I was just out for a walk," he said through the pain in his arm.

That's when a porch light came on and a man came out the door with a rifle. I knew him through Diane.

"Who's out there?" he called.

"It's Cam Derringer, Bill. I found this guy snooping around."

"You got 'im?"

"Yeah."

"We've had some trouble lately. Peepin' Tom. Stole some stuff from my garage a few days ago too. I'll call the police."

I held him in place and Walter didn't leave the guy until the police came.

"I'll leave it to you now," I said and turned to leave.

"Can you come to the station in the morning? We'll need a statement from you," one of the policemen said.

"Sure," I said and left. But I wasn't sure I was going to be at the station in the morning; however, I knew Bill would be there.

Back at Diane's house I petted Walter and gave him a good back rub. He was a blessing to me. I was more worried he'd get hurt than I was about my own safety. Something that any good pet owner experiences.

That's when I decided that first thing in the morning I was going to get Diane an alarm and camera for her house. This is a dangerous world we live in nowadays. I only hope something big changes in the near future to make times better.

I asked Walter if he was ready to turn in. Of course, he didn't answer me again. This dog doesn't talk much, even though he says a lot.

John Bexley arrived in Key West at eight thirty-five p.m. He checked into the Doubletree resort. The room was more luxurious than he was used to since he didn't need to worry about what he spent anymore. Being a millionaire definitely had its advantages.

He ordered room service. When the T-bone arrived with a bottle of Scotch, he tipped the girl fifty dollars and asked her to tell anyone who inquired that he wasn't there.

"You've got it, sir. Anything else?"

Although there was something he'd like to have had from the young cutie, he said, "No, thank you."

"My pleasure," she said and left the room.

"Yes, it would be your pleasure," John said when she was gone.

He ate his steak, showered, and got into bed. He turned on the TV for white noise while he tried to go to sleep. When he heard the name Cam Derringer on the TV, he sat up in bed and grabbed the remote. He turned up the volume and listened.

"Tomorrow, at eleven thirty, Cam Derringer will recall his heroic adventure during our Murder Fest Key West convention two years ago. This is one you don't want to miss, especially if you live here. Most of you will remember the gruesome murders that took place..."

Bexley turned the TV down and smiled to himself. "Got ya."

Chapter 14

Stan and Holly pulled into Ocean's Edge Resort and Marina at Key West at nine-thirty. They docked the boat.

They had already removed all the new numbers. The boat was now the way it was when he rented it.

"We've got a room here," Stan said. "215."

"We'll rent a car and visit Cam in a few minutes. We need to stash these clothes on his skiff."

"That sounds like a plan. The icing on the cake."

They drove their rental to the docks and shut off the lights. They watched the boats for a few minutes before deciding no one was around.

"You wait here. Keep your gun handy," Stan said.

He exited the car and walked to the docks. They seemed to be right. No one was there.

He stashed the plastic bag with Cam's and Stacy's clothes in it in the livewell and walked back to the car.

"Let's get some sleep. In the morning, we'll visit Cam's boat again. Bexley will be around here somewhere."

"Sounds good. You still owe me something."

"First thing in the morning," he said.

"It's almost morning now."

"You're insatiable aren't you?"

"Yep."

Stan laughed and kissed her.

The sun was up already when I woke. I was surprised I'd slept so late. I looked down at the floor to see Walter lying asleep on his back.

That fight must have worn him out. As soon as I stepped out of bed he rolled over and jumped up.

I turned on the coffee and let Walter out into the backyard. I gave him food and water. He'd been so tired he didn't even hide his bowl before he went to sleep.

I turned on the news while I drank my coffee. There was another story about the shooting at Sombrero but nothing new. So far, no one had come forward with a video.

John Bexley arrived at the World's End Resort at eight thirty a.m. to get a ticket for the afternoon conference and workshop where Cam was going to give a speech.

He walked around the area to find the best location to view Cam on stage. He found a spot backstage that offered a good shot and an immediate escape. He wasn't worried about the other members of the author group who would be hanging out back there. As soon as he shot Cam, they would run in the opposite direction. Plus, he'd wear a COVID mask. In and out, ten minutes.

"Cam Derringer?" the woman on the phone asked.

"That depends. Who am I speaking with?"

"A friend who wants to keep you out of trouble."

"What kind of trouble could I possibly be in?" I asked, already knowing the answer.

She laughed softly and seductively. "I was at the beach yesterday," she said. "I saw you there."

"I wasn't at Smathers Beach yesterday," I said, playing cat and mouse.

"Sombrero."

"I wasn't there either."

"The beach cam film begs to differ."

"Ah, so you have the beach cam film. How's the quality?"

"Good enough. I'd like to give it to you."

"I'm not sure I would want it, but I'll bet ya the police would like to have it."

"You're playing a very dangerous game with me, Cam. I'll give it to them."

"Okay," I said and hung up.

I called her bluff and hoped it wasn't a mistake. The phone rang again. I let it ring four times before I answered it.

"Hello."

"You could be in big trouble."

"Who is this?"

"I want two hundred thousand in twenties by tomorrow morning or the tape goes to the police."

"I'm not sure you have what you think you have. As I said, I wasn't at Sombrero yesterday."

"You might be able to handle the trouble, but do you think little Stacy can?"

I hesitated a bit then said, "Send me a copy of what you have; then I'll let you know if I want to buy it."

"Oh, you'll want to buy it. There's a copy on Diane's front porch right now."

I stood and walked to the front door. When I opened it, I found a package between the door and the screen door.

I picked it up and took it into the house. She was still on the phone. "I'll call you back in a half-hour. Enjoy the movie."

"Wait, how did you get this movie? I know people who are looking for it and they are not going to be happy that you stole it."

"Losers weepers," she said and hung up.

Who the hell was that and how'd she get this?

I took the thumb drive out of the white envelope and slid it into Diane's laptop.

It was basically the same as the one I have but the camera didn't move. The wide angle of the lens caught the whole thing though. When they turned the boat to leave, I used my fingers to zoom in. The boat was just like Diane's right down to the name on the back and the numbers.

I called Malinda and told her about the blackmail. She told me to set up whatever it would take to deliver the money and she'd make sure someone was there to catch the girl.

"How do you explain this, Cam?"

"I tell you, it wasn't us."

"I know that, but who was it? What did you do to someone now?"

"You know who was behind this. Camata and Bexley. They both want me dead or in prison."

I heard Malinda sigh. "Probably so. I'll have someone check on Camata. Meantime, Bexley is more than likely in Key West and looking for you. Be careful and protect Stacy too."

"I'm trying. The thing is someone was hired to kill Bexley and failed. They're going to have to go after him. My guess is Camata hired them. You know, an assassin who resembles me. They could change their looks a little. I noticed the guy even favored his right side a little like I do."

"I'll see what more I can find out. Call me back after you talk to the girl again."

When we were finished talking, I got Walter and drove down to Duval Street. I wished Jack was there. If I was going to put myself out in the open, I'd have liked a backup.

The streets were already starting to fill with tourists. It was another beautiful, hot, muggy day. I walked into the Hog's Breath Saloon and took a stool at the bar.

I knew this bar was a little out of the way. I didn't really think someone would find me there. But if they were following me, this was the perfect spot. The street was narrow and I had a good view of it from the stool. If someone did want to take a shot at me, they'd have to be close and there wasn't a great escape route.

I ordered a Coke and a donut. Walter ordered water and a donut. I knew what he would want.

We sat there for a few minutes before my phone rang.

I answered but didn't say anything.

"Okay, Cam, what's it gonna be?"

"Do you mean am I going to give you two hundred thousand dollars?"

"Yes, that's what I mean."

"No, I'll give you one hundred thousand." I wanted her to think I was going to do the deal but wanted to haggle a little.

"I thought you might say something like that. You can add that one hundred thousand to the original two hundred thousand and now bring me three hundred thousand."

"That's not the way it works."

"It does now. What do ya say, you want to go to jail or do you want to lose a small bit of your fortune?"

"When and where?" I finally relented.

"I'll call you later with the details. Meantime, go get the money."

"When will you call me?"

"When you have the money, and, Cam, those donuts are bad for your health," she said and hung up.

I took a quick look around the area but didn't see anyone suspicious. She was following me. If she could do it, someone else could too.

Chapter 15

Stan and Holly were up and dressed at eight. They had a long night of lovemaking and had slept in. Holly's hair was brown again. The wig hung on the bathroom hook.

"That was exhausting," she said. "I'm starving."

"We can get a bite downstairs. Then we need to stake out Cam's boat and wait for Bexley to show up."

"Why don't we just take Cam out? We can always find Bexley."

"It has to look like Bexley is the one who killed Cam or make it look like Cam killed all those people on the beach so he'll go to prison."

"Whatever. I think Camata's too afraid of Brittany."

"From what I hear, he better be. Let's go."

While they were eating they watched the news in the buffet room. It was mostly about the massacre at Sombrero Beach. It appeared they didn't have a clue as to who the shooters were. Then a picture of Cam Derringer came on the screen and a man said Cam would be speaking at the MFKW conference that day.

"Now we know where we can find him. And what happened to the beach cams?" Holly asked. "They were supposed to catch everything."

"Yeah, they were working the day before. I tuned into them and watched the people on the beach from my phone."

"We need to visit their Chamber of Commerce. Someone's holding out."

They finished eating and rented a car. They drove to Blue Harbour Point.

After sitting in the parking lot for a half-hour, Holly said, "Fuck this shit. I'm not going to sit around here and twiddle my thumbs."

She opened the car door and got out.

"Where do you think you're going? We can catch him at the conference," Stan yelled.

"I'm gonna go see Cam!"

With that, she walked to the dock and opened the gate. She was almost to Cam's boat when Stacy called, "Can I help you?"

Holly froze then turned around. She smiled. "Maybe, I'm looking for Cam Derringer. Does he live here?"

"What do you want with him?" Stacy asked suspiciously.

"I would like to hire him. My friend has been missing for three days."

"I don't think he's taking any jobs right now. If you leave me your number, I'll give it to him. He'll call you either way."

"He isn't home then?"

"No, he's been gone all day. Haven't I seen you somewhere?" Stacy asked.

"I don't think so," Holly answered, making it obvious that she was trying to remember. "Hey, aren't you a waitress at Coyote Ugly?"

Stacy smiled. "Yeah. I guess I saw you there."

"Small world."

"Yep. Do you want me to have him call you?"

"I don't know. I don't want to bother 'im if he's not taking any cases."

"Just a second," Stacy said. She stepped inside her boat and returned with one of Cam's business cards. "Here ya go. Give him a call."

"Will do. Thank you," Holly said and walked back toward the gate.

"I hope you find your friend!" Stacy called.

Holly waved back over her shoulder.

"What was that all about?" Stan asked when she got in the car.

"Stacy stopped me. Cam's not home anyway."

"What were you going to do if he was home?"

"I don't know for sure. On the way up there, I thought about maybe killing him."

"That would be the worst thing you could have done."

"Shit," Holly said. "Get down."

Stan looked behind him and saw three black SUVs fly into the parking lot. He ducked down in the seat with Holly.

"CIA," Holly said.

"Yeah, I think so. I guess the tapes got out there."

Once the agents were out of their car and walking toward the dock, Stan started the car and eased out of the lot.

Stacy was sitting on her lanai watching the ten agents coming toward her boat. "What the hell?" she said out loud.

The first one stopped at her gangway. "Stacy Monroe?" he asked.

She nodded but was too frightened to speak. He turned toward the second man and nodded his head toward Stacy.

The man came on board and told her to stand. He spun her around and handcuffed her and then read her her rights.

The others went on toward Cam's boat.

"He's not home," Stacy said.

They didn't slow down. They rushed the boat and broke the door in. Five of the agents stood on the dock and the deck of the boat while the others went in, guns drawn.

They returned and stood on the bow while they discussed whatever. Then they all looked at Stacy and started walking toward her.

"What's this all about?" she asked.

"Shut up and sit down. Is this your boat?" the agent asked, pointing at Diane's skiff.

"I've never seen that boat before," she said.

"Yeah, right. Search it," he commanded.

Two of the agents climbed onto the boat and ransacked it. One of them held up a plastic bag.

"Clothes!" he yelled.

"Bring 'em here," said the agent in charge.

He took the bag and emptied it onto Stacy's table.

When she saw her clothes and some of Cam's fall onto the table, she knew she was in big trouble.

'Take 'er in," he said. "Carson, you and Talbert stay here in your car. When Cam comes home, get 'im."

My cell rang again. "Hello, Ma... Brittany," I said after I caught myself.

"It doesn't matter what you call me, Cam. We're secure."

"My phone might not be."

"It is. It was checked before it rang."

"Oh, so what's up?"

"Did you get the money and talk to the woman yet?"

"I talked to her. I struck a deal that only cost me another one hundred thousand."

"You're good. Listen carefully. Don't take any more calls from her. She's with the CIA. They were baiting you. Once you agreed to buy the tape, they knew you had something to hide. They stole the tape from one of my guys. Eric. Now you're a wanted man. And, I'm afraid, Stacy is wanted too."

"Can't you do something about the CIA? You work with them and you know we're innocent."

"Maybe I can later, but right now they're in a frenzy. They think they've broken the biggest case of the century wide open. We have to prove them wrong."

"What if we can't?"

"We don't want to think about that. Kailey will be there late today."

"Jack and Diane will be here too. It's her boat that's in the tape. At least one that looks like hers."

"Warn them and check on Stacy. You're all in trouble. I'm on my way there."

"Thanks."

After we hung up I called Ryan Chase.

"Hey, Ryan, is Stacy still with you?"

"No, Cam, I took her home this morning. What the hell have you two done?"

"We haven't done anything, but we're in big trouble. Someone has set us up."

"I hope you're right. I'm looking at Stacy right now. She's being printed and readied for her cell. They found her clothes and yours in a plastic bag in the skiff. They are the same clothes from the beach murders."

I felt like I'd been punched in the stomach. "Don't let them hurt her. She was with me, scuba diving, when all that took place."

"I believe you, Cam, but I can't do much."

"You can look for Bexley. He's a part of this. Someone was trying to kill him and make it look like it was me doing it."

"Okay, I'll do what I can, I know what he looks like, but I'm not going to tell everyone I'm doing this for you."

"Thanks, Ryan. If you get a chance, tell Stacy I'll be there for her as soon as I can."

My next call was to Jack. I really dreaded this one. Diane thought she couldn't leave without me getting into some kind of trouble. Maybe she was right.

"Hey Jack, where are you guys?"

"We're just pulling into Florida City. Why? What did you do?"

"Put it on speaker," I heard Diane say.

I wanted to say, "I didn't do anything," but I didn't have time to argue with them.

"Well, we have a problem here," I said and then went through the whole story. "And it is Diane's boat that they found the clothes in. You can't bring her back here right now. Drop her off at John James' house in Marathon. I'll call him and arrange it."

Diane said, "I knew I shouldn't have gone away. You can't be trusted for one week."

"This wasn't me, Diane. This was Camata and the man who tried to kill me once before. You remember him, don't you? The guy you were shooting at from my boat two months ago."

She could hear the anger in my voice. She said, "You're right, Cam. Sorry. What can we do to help?"

"You need to stay away from Key West until we get this straightened out. I would like Jack's help though. Kailey will be here tonight and Malinda said she's on her way. I'm kinda tied down as to what I can do. They're looking for me now."

"I can be there in about four hours," Jack said. "I'll get Diane a hotel in Key Largo. I don't want John to get in any trouble. Besides, he only lives two blocks from Sombrero Beach. The cops might be knocking on doors."

"Yeah, you're right. Call me when you get here."

"Where will you stay until then?"

"I'm supposed to give a speech at noon for the Murder Fest Key West conference. It's a cinch I can't do that, but it's been on the news. I think Bexley might show up there, or the guy who impersonated me. I'm going to find a disguise and go to the parking lot."

"That sounds dangerous. I can probably be there before the conference lets out," Jack said. "I'll call you."

Chapter 16

Malinda stepped off her private jet in Key West at ten fifteen. As she was about to get into her limo, a man put his hand on the door.

"Brittany Pierce?" he asked.

One glance at him told her he was with the CIA. She hadn't called for any backup. What did he want?

"Yes."

"I'm afraid you're going to have to come with me."

"What's this about? You do know who I am, right?"

"Yes, ma'am. I'm just following orders."

"Where are you taking me?"

"To a safe house."

"I don't need a safe house. I'm capable of taking care of myself in any situation."

"I know that, but we can't let you contact Cam Derringer. We know you have a history with him."

"I wouldn't want to be you when I'm free," she said harshly.

"Yes, ma'am."

She went with him and two other agents to their car. They drove out of the airport and north on the Overseas Highway. She didn't speak to them again until they opened the door and let her out in front of a Quonset hut at the Key West Naval Air Station.

The Quonset hut wasn't marked. The exterior was rusty and the wooden door was covered with chipped paint that might have been green at one time.

An agent opened the door and she stepped inside. The interior was as brilliant as the exterior was rundown. TV monitors lined the walls each showing a different spot around Key West. Men were standing around a large table in the center of the room and four desks were positioned near each corner.

A fit, handsome man turned toward her when she entered. He smiled and came to her. "Brittany, it's good to see you again."

She wasn't amused. "What's this all about, Marcello?"

He got a disappointed look on his face. "I was hoping you'd be happy to see me again."

"Maybe so, under different circumstances."

"Come here, I want to show you something."

She walked to the table with him and looked down at another monitor. It was showing Sombrero Beach and the gunfight.

"I've seen it," she said.

"Then you know what Cam has done."

"That's not Cam," she said.

"Really? Well, the man he was trying to kill sure thought he was."

When the time came, he turned up the speaker. "Cam!" Bexley said on the tape.

"Yeah, the guy fooled him, but he can't fool me. That's not Cam."

He pointed to another figure in the film. "See that guy?" he said, just as the man was shot and fell to the ground. "That was one of our best undercover agents. Cam shot him. He's dead. Someone's going to pay."

"Someone should pay. But not Cam. He wasn't there."

"That guy, Bexley, we know he was the one who tried to kill Cam a few months ago. Cam came to seek revenge and got carried away."

The film looked damning even to Brittany. It was hard to argue.

"I know it wasn't Cam. Give me a chance to find the real assassin."

"We have the real assassins. Cam Derringer and Stacy Monroe. The clothes they were wearing in the film—" he stopped and pointed at the film "—those clothes right there, we found in Cam's skiff. How do you explain that?"

"He was set up. It would be easy."

"No, not so easy. I'm afraid, Brit, we're going to have to detain you while we search for Cam. You're a threat to the investigation."

Brittany looked around the room and studied all the faces. Each man she stared at looked away. Her reputation was one of handling situations with force and usually termination.

"You're going to be sorry when this is over," she said calmly to Marcello.

"I doubt it," he rebutted.

I couldn't go back to Diane's house now. I wondered if the woman on the phone was still following me.

I pulled into Garrison Bight with Walter and parked. I waited a few minutes watching the entrance. When no one came in, we got out and ran to Jack's skiff. I found the keys where he hides them under the back seat and started the boat. Walter jumped in and crouched low. I think he understood that we were in a jam. This wasn't his first rodeo.

I pulled out of the Bight and into the gulf. Now where was I going to go? I didn't have a plan. I turned north and cruised through Flemming Cut until I found myself pulling into Barnacle Jill's Dive Shop. Jill was standing on the dock smoking a cigarette. She watched me pull up to the dock and reached out for the line. I tossed it to her and she tied me off.

As I stepped onto the dock, she asked, "Kill anyone else today?"

I was stunned for an instant. "What?"

"It's all over the news now. You're in some deep shit."

I felt my shoulders slump. "Sorry," I said and turned to get back in the boat.

"Where the hell you goin'?"

"I can't stay here and endanger you."

"Bullshit," she said and tossed her cigarette into a bucket. "Come on inside. You need a place to hide."

Walter and I followed her to the shop. Once inside she turned and locked the door and flipped the open sign around so it read, "Closed."

"What are ya gonna do, Cam?"

"I don't know. I have some help coming later today, but until then I was just trying to stay out of sight."

"Where'd you go diving yesterday?"

"Joe's Barge," I said.

"Surely someone saw you there."

"I don't remember seeing another boat in the area other than a cruiser a couple of hundred yards away. But I never saw a diver."

"That's unusual."

"Yeah, I thought so too. The boat had out a line of buoys like he was closing down the area, but he let us slip right through."

"That sounds suspicious in itself," she said.

"You're right, it does."

"Someone got you good. You can stay here as long as you want. When a customer comes in, you can hide in my bedroom in the back."

"Thanks, Jill, but I have things I need to check on. If I don't find who did this, they'll catch me sooner or later."

"If they catch you, you'll never have a chance to find 'em. Take a break and I'll go to Salties and get us something to eat. What you want?"

"Are you and Aaron on good terms?"

"We were when he left here this mornin'."

I waggled my finger at her. She waved me off and actually blushed.

"I'll have a chili dog and fries," I said.

"Be right back," she said; then she turned and left.

She didn't shut the door. I crossed the room to close it. As I was about to push it closed a beautiful Bahamian woman stepped in. I hadn't seen her boat pull up so she must have come by car. Her clothing didn't give her away, but I'd spent enough time in the Bahamas to know she was from there.

"We're closed," I said. "Can you come back in an hour?"

"Brittany got arrested," she said. "CIA. She won't be helping you."

I just stared at her for a minute trying to comprehend. "Brittany was arrested?"

"Yes. I am Lydia. I was on the plane with her."

"Why was she arrested?" I asked her.

"They don't want her to help you."

I hesitated but then said, "Come in."

She came in and I closed the door.

"How did you know where I was?"

She pulled out a small black box from her pocket and flipped it on. The screen lit up and showed a concentrated area of Key West. It was positioned over a four-block area in which we were in the center. A red dot in the center of the screen was blinking. It was a GPS tracker.

"So, I have a tracker on me somewhere?"

She smiled and looked at Walter. She nodded to him. He just stared back at her. "Him," she said. "His collar."

Then it hit me. Malinda had given him the collar for Christmas the previous year. She had placed a tracking chip in it. These women are way too overprotective of me.

"How are you going to help me? Do you know who the assassin is?"

"I'm not sure, but I think I have an idea. We studied the film. There is a slight resemblance to a man who started in the business about five years ago. The film from the beach cam is a little blurry, but it might be him."

"Yeah, Stan Whittle," I said.

"She told you?"

I nodded.

Just then the door opened. Lydia spun around and at the same time raised a gun at the door. Where the gun came from I don't know. Jill raised her hand in front of her and said, "Whoa there, girl. I'm a friend."

Lydia saw that it was the woman who was here a few minutes ago and lowered the gun. "Sorry," she said.

I could see that Lydia was probably capable of protecting me. But I'm not sure that I want another woman in my life, especially another dangerous woman.

Jill came in and placed a sack on the counter. "Eat up," she said. And looking at Lydia she said, "I didn't know you were here or I would have brought you something to eat too."

"I'm good," Lydia said.

I didn't move toward the food. My attention was on Lydia.

"I don't want you with me. I can move more freely alone," I told her.

"As you wish. I only came to tell you about Brittany."

"Thank you," I said.

She nodded at me, turned, and left the store.

"She's a friendly one," Jill said.

"Yeah."

I ate my chili dog and told Jill thanks. "I'll see you soon, I hope."

"You can stay here anytime you need to. The key's under that rock over there," she said, pointing.

Walter and I walked to the boat and untied it. I pushed off and we idled away. My watch said ten fifty. It was time to go get the car and head to the parking lot at the hotel. Maybe Bexley would show up.

Chapter 17

I thought about leaving Walter at Jack's boat but then figured I might not be able to come back and get him. We climbed in the car and headed for the World's End Resort.

The lot was crowded. However, we did find someone pulling out of the front row on the right end of the lot where we could watch the entrance.

It was, of course, another hot, muggy day, so, for Walter, I left the engine running and turned on the AC. We watched the crowd walk into the lobby. Some of them, I knew were coming to listen to me. I wasn't going to be there. Anyone who knew what was going on would be able to figure that out. Even so, I saw six policemen walk in, and a few minutes later, a CIA car stopped at the entrance and three suited men got out and entered.

"Those guys are here for us," I told Walter.

He watched them curiously. Did he know what was happening? I know sometimes he can sense these things and other times he's just plain weird.

I jumped when someone knocked on my window. I turned to look. It was Lydia. I unlocked the door and she climbed in. Walter slipped through the seats to the back to give her room.

"You shouldn't be here," she said. "It's dangerous."

"Yeah, I know, but if I'm going to find whoever killed those people, I might have to live dangerously."

"I'll watch for them. You leave now."

"No. I'm going to stay here too. You can go inside and take a look. I'll stay out here and watch the lot. The place is filled with cops and CIA."

"I saw them," she said, looking around the lot. "I heard from Kailey a few minutes ago. She'll be here in about an hour."

That ran a bolt of relief through my body. She was someone I would and could trust with my life. And I miss her when she's gone.

"Good. Will she know where to find me?"

"She'll know. Be careful out here," she said, opening the door. "I'll call you if I see anyone."

When she was gone, I thought I had better call Jack to let him know I was there.

"We're about an hour away," he said.

"We?"

"You know Diane. You try to stop 'er."

"I'm okay, Cam. I can take care of myself," I heard her say.

"Don't go home. You can stay at Jack's boat or his house."

"Okay, Cam," she said, but I knew she'd do whatever she wanted to do.

"I'm at the World's End. I want Jack to come here alone. Kailey will be here about the same time."

"I'll be there," Jack said.

After we hung up, I watched the building again. At five minutes till twelve, I saw a man walk in the side entrance. He was large and wore a ball cap pulled down to shade his eyes. There was no doubt that he was John Bexley.

I wanted to call Lydia, but I didn't get her number. I checked the lot and got out of the car. I cracked the window first and let the AC run for Walter.

When I reached the side door, I opened it slowly. My eyes were still trying to recover from the sun. I couldn't see very well inside. I stopped at the door and waited a few seconds for them to adjust. When they did, Bexley was only ten feet in front of me. He held a gun in his hand and it was pointed right at me.

"Hello, Cam. It's a good day to die."

I froze. My gun was still in my belt. There was no way I could reach it before he blew me away.

"It wasn't me at the beach, John. It was Stan Whittle. Camata hired him to kill you and make it look like it was me."

Bexley stood still for a few seconds then said, "Thanks for the info. I'll kill them after I kill you," he said and raised his gun.

"Cam!" Henry Tally called from behind Bexley. "I didn't think you were going to make it."

Bexley turned. It gave me enough time to pull my gun out of my belt and fire a shot into Bexley's shoulder. He dropped his gun. I rushed him and hit him hard in the jaw. He went down. I picked up his gun.

"Here, hold this," I told Henry, handing him the gun. "The CIA are inside. Tell them this is John Bexley. They're looking for him."

I didn't wait for a response. I turned and ran out the side door. When I reached the car, I heard another shot. I turned to look back. Lydia was standing at the open door. Then she disappeared back inside.

I put the car in gear and tore out of the lot. *Why did she go back in?*

Stan and Holly heard the shot at the same time everyone else did. Seconds later, they heard another shot. They stood aside as people ran from the lobby and out the front door.

"Let's go check it out," Holly said.

They went to the back of the room and peeked around the corner. A man came screaming out of the room with a gun in his hand. He was yelling, "Help!"

They saw Bexley lying on the floor in a puddle of blood.

"I think he's dead. Did that guy shoot him?" Stan asked.

"I don't know, but we need to get the hell out of here. I'll bet Cam shot 'im."

"Out of the way," a man said from behind them. "You folks get out of here."

He was a CIA agent no doubt. Stan and Holly turned and left with the remaining crowd.

I called Jack back and told him to stay away from the hotel. "I'll meet you at your boat," I said. "I just shot Bexley."

"Is he dead?"

"No, I left him for the CIA."

I was only five minutes away from his boat. Several police cars and an ambulance passed me on the way.

Shit, I was in big trouble now. I might have been able to get out of the beach murders, but there was an eyewitness to me shooting Bexley in the arm.

I turned into the marina and parked between two other cars in the more crowded area of the lot. I decided to wait in the car.

Fifteen minutes later, I saw Jack and Diane pull into the lot. They parked in front of Jack's boat and walked to the dock. Jack disappeared inside then returned to the bow and looked around. I called him.

"I'm in the lot. A brown Chevy SUV." When he looked my way, I flashed the lights.

"Tell Diane to get in your skiff and push her off. If the police show up, tell her to go to Jill's Dive Shop and wait."

"Do you really think that's necessary?"

"I don't know, but I'd rather be safe."

I saw him turn and say something to Diane. She looked my way and raised her arms in protest but went to the boat anyway. Jack pushed her off and I heard the engine fire up.

"Okay, Cam. She's safe. Now, what happened?"

"I saw Bexley going into the hotel; I followed him in and we both had guns. I shot him in the arm and left."

"Any witnesses?"

"Yeah, Henry, the Fest chairman. I gave him Bexley's gun and told him to get the CIA. When I left, I heard another shot."

"Damn, Cam. What were you thinking?"

"I was thinking it was either him or me. Last time, it was me."

"Come on in my boat. We'll figure this out together."

"There was a woman there too. Her name is Lydia. She came to Jill's place to tell me Malinda had been arrested by the CIA. After I left Bexley, she went back inside."

"We can't worry about her now. Come on in."

I opened the car door to get out. Walter leaped over me and ran toward Jack. Before I could close the door, a police car turned into the lot and went straight to Jack's boat. Its lights were flashing.

"Walter!" I yelled.

He stopped and turned to look at me. Then he looked at the police car and back at me again. When he saw me getting back into the car he turned and ran toward me. Luckily, the police must not have seen him. He jumped into the front seat.

I turned to look at Diane. She was motoring out of the Bight. *Good girl.*

My car door flew open again.

Chapter 18

Kailey leaned across the seat and kissed me. "Let's get out of here. We'll take my car," she said. She turned in the seat and patted Walter on the head. He was as excited to see her as I was.

The three of us stayed low behind the cars and got into her Mercedes.

"Where are we going?" I asked.

"The Galleon."

"That's not safe. There's only one way in and one way out."

"Yeah, if you're in a car. On foot, you're free to go wherever. In a boat, the world is your playground."

"I've forgotten how poetic you are."

"I'll remind you as soon as we get in the room."

When we pulled into the lot off Front Street, I saw a man watching us carefully. Then he turned to another man further down the lot and waved.

"It's a trap," I said.

"They're with me. Calm down."

We parked in a spot in front of the B building and took the back steps to the third floor. When we entered the room, a man handed her the key and left. I walked to the back of the condo and looked out. The whole back of the room was open to the marina. "Wow, what a view."

"Thank you," I heard her say.

I turned to see Naked Kailey, as I call her, well, naked. What a lovely sight she is.

"Really?" I said.

"We have time," she said and put her arms around me.

We did have time.

We were lying on the bed naked when I heard a knock at the door.

"Come in," Kailey said.

Lydia entered the room and came over to the bed. She didn't pay any attention to us being naked, but I felt a little uneasy. Kailey could tell.

"He's such a prude," she said and the girls both giggled.

"Okay, okay, what's going on here?" I asked.

"Did you get him?" Kailey asked.

"The CIA have 'im."

"Who?" I asked.

"Bexley."

"He was alive when I left him. The CIA was going to get 'im," I said.

"He's still alive," Lydia said.

"They'll know I did it."

"Didn't you?' she asked.

"I shot him in the shoulder. He was alive."

Lydia looked at Kailey then back at me.

"Well, he's still alive, so quit worrying."

I was still feeling a little uncomfortable lying there naked in front of someone I didn't know.

Lydia looked down at my cock and then back at Kailey. She smiled and said, "I thought you were lying."

Kailey smiled. I covered myself with my hands. "Let's get back to business."

"All three of us?" Kailey said sensuously.

"Not that business. I'm in serious trouble and so are Diane and Stacy."

"Diane's okay. We have her in sight. She'll be picked up by some of our people," Lydia said.

"Some of our people?" I asked.

"Don't worry about Stacy. She's being taken good care of. When we find the two assassins, she'll be free."

I got out of bed and picked up my clothes. When I turned around, both girls were looking at me and smiling.

"For heaven's sake, girls," I said and slipped on my shorts.

Walter came into the bedroom now sensing the intimacy was over. He got pets and hugs from both girls.

"What's the plan?" I asked.

"I'm going to End of the World to check the security tapes. I know Stan had to be there. I want to see who the girl he was working with is," Kailey said.

"And you?" I said, turning to Lydia.

"I'm going back to Bahama now. My work is finished here, unless..." she said, looking back down at my cock again.

They laughed. I felt used.

Lydia kissed me on the cheek. "Next time," she said and kissed Kailey. "See you soon, I hope," she said and went to the door.

"Will you be okay?" I asked.

"I'll be okay."

When she was gone, Kailey said she'd be back in a few minutes.

"How do you think you're going to get those tapes?" I asked.

"I know a guy," she said.

I had forgotten whom I was talking to. She always knew a guy.

When Kailey left the condo, I stepped onto the rear deck and called Jack.

"Are they gone?" I asked.

"Yeah, they were looking for you. So far they haven't mentioned Diane."

"Bexley's in custody. Lydia said he'd been arrested by the CIA. At least I don't have to worry about him anymore."

"Have you heard from Kailey?"

"Oh, yeah. She was in the parking lot. We're at the Galleon. She's gone now to get the surveillance camera from the World's End Resort. She thinks she might be able to find the assassins."

"Good luck. Do you want me to come there?"

"Not yet. The police might be watching you. I'll call you late this evening though."

"Call me right away if, and when, you get in trouble. I'll be there."

"Thanks. Have you heard from Diane?"

"She's at Jill's. They're going to Salties to eat. That place is so far off the grid no one will see her there."

"You should probably stay away from her for a while too."

"Will do."

We hung up and I finished getting dressed. I wanted to get back on the street. I might just flush out the assassins myself.

When I opened the door, a man stopped me. "Sorry, Cam. Kailey said for you to stay put. She'll be back in an hour or so. Can we get you anything?"

"No, I'm good," I said and went back inside.

But I wasn't good. I went to the veranda and stepped out to the railing. Three floors up. Shit. There was a tree that reached all the way to the balcony below me. If I could get down to it, I could easily manage to get to the ground.

I climbed over the rail and lowered myself to where I hung by my hands from the floor of my deck. I took two big swings and let go. I managed to land on the floor below me. I didn't know if anyone was in that room but I wasn't going to wait around to find out. I turned and grabbed a tree branch and swung toward the trunk. If anyone had seen me, they'd have thought I was a cat burglar. Once I was secure in the tree, I began my descent. It was only a two-foot drop from the bottom branch.

I brushed myself off and walked along the boardwalk toward Schooner's Bar. I had friends there.

Stan and Holly were heading back toward Garrison Bight where they had left the boat.

On the way, Stan called Camata. "Bexley is dead. Cam is nowhere to be found. I think he's the one who shot him."

"Do the police know he's the one who shot him?"

"No idea. I'm just telling you what I know."

"Oh, is that what you know? What I know is I paid you to either kill Cam Derringer or make sure he spends the rest of his life in prison. Which one has happened?"

"Neither yet, but it will. It's just going to take a little longer than I thought."

"Starting today, every day costs you fifty thousand dollars."

"That's bullshit. This isn't your normal hit. Hello ... hello. Shit, he hung up on me."

"Did you expect him to be happy?"

"He said that every day Cam lives will cost me fifty thousand. Let's go. I'm gonna kill him today."

"Where are we going?"

"Everywhere he goes. His boat, his daughters, his friends, the fuckin' grocery store," he yelled and slammed his fist on the dashboard. "Everywhere!"

"Let's turn on the handheld. We'll monitor the police and get to him before they can," Holly said pulling it out of her purse.

I took a stool at the bar in Schooners. Sammy was rolling cigars. He stopped long enough to give me a smile and a wink. I pulled my ball cap down further to hide my face. He nodded. Then his bird, Pirate, screamed, "Cam!"

I cringed. Sammy put his hand over Pirate's mouth. Everyone just laughed. They didn't know he was hollering at me. They'd probably never even heard of me. When tourists come to Key West, they don't spend much time watching TV.

Dave was bartending. I didn't even know he was in town. The last time I saw him, he brought Walter's son to see him.

"Cam, my man. How's it hangin'?" Dave said with a slur.

"What's up, Dave? When did you get into town?"

"Last night. Came here this morning and got my job back."

"And Wanda?" I asked.

Wanda jumped up from behind the bar right in front of me. "Surprise!" she yelled with her hands in the air.

Of all the places I could come to be inconspicuous, I came here.

"Hey Wanda," I said as low-key as I could.

She replied by pulling her top up and flashing me. Now everyone in the bar was looking at us. Dave laughed.

"It was good to see you two," I said as I stood. "Wish I could hang around for a while." I turned to leave.

"Cam," Wanda said quietly, "if you need a place to stay, we're back in the same house we were in last year. The key's under the mat."

"Thanks, Wanda," I said and left.

Maybe being out in the open wasn't such a good idea. I was a sitting duck out there. I decided to go to Jack's boat. He was probably back at his house by now. I wondered if anyone had picked Diane up yet. I called her cell.

"Hello," she answered. She has caller ID and never answers with hello.

"Are you okay?"

"You'll have to call the office to make an appointment. They'll be in tomorrow morning."

"Are you safe?"

"Yes, that would be fine. Thank you," she said and hung up.

The police must have found her wherever she was. I called Jack. "Have you spoken to Diane?"

"I have eyes on her now. She's sitting in Salties. Two police are questioning her. They probably don't know it was her boat or they would have taken her in by now. I guess the CIA isn't sharing that bit of info."

"Probably not. I'm headed to your boat. Is that okay?"

"Sure, but what about Kailey?"

"Some things I need to do on my own."

"Be careful, Cam. Things don't always turn out for the best when you do things on your own."

"Name one time."

"I don't have time for all the times so I'll just use the last one when you were killed."

"Never mind. I'll talk to you later," I said and hung up.

I didn't want to be in the crowd any longer so I took the back way out of Schooners. As I was leaving I heard someone yell, "Hey, it's the guy from the TV. The one they're looking for. He killed some people in Marathon."

I turned to look back. Everyone was looking at me. I took off running down William Street and cut through the Key West Bight parking lot. I turned up Margaret Street, ran to Eaton, turned, and ran to Betty's Bakery. I pushed the door open just as a police car, sirens wailing, passed the shop.

There were two patrons buying donuts when I entered. I took a seat at a window table and waited for them to leave.

When they were gone, Betty said, "You really did it this time, Cam. You're all over the TV and I guess that police car that just passed is after you."

"I didn't do anything, Betty. I'm being framed. I'll be out of here in just a minute," I said, looking out the window.

"Get your ass into the back room and don't come out until I tell ya to."

"Thank you," I said and walked to the door leading to the kitchen.

"And don't be eating all my donuts."

"Yes, ma'am."

"Where did you leave Walter?"

"The Galleon."

"Has he got food and water?"

"He does."

"Give me five minutes to close up and I'll take you there. You can lie on my back seat."

"Betty, you don't have to do that," I said.

"Look at all those times you gave me free advice and then helped me out in court. You charged me nothin'. This is the least I can do."

I nodded to her, took a seat on her baking stool, and ate a chocolate honeybun.

Chapter 19

Diane was still sitting at Salties with Jill fifteen minutes after the police left. A man and woman entered the bar. They weren't dressed as if they hung out there. The woman had on white slacks and a blue blouse and the man was wearing a suit. It was fitted and looked very expensive.

They looked around the room and their gaze landed on Diane. She watched as they walked toward her.

"Diane," the woman said, "we are here for you."

"What do you mean you're here for me?"

"Kailey wants you to come with us."

"Just a minute," Diane said and dialed Kailey's private number.

"Hi Diane, are you okay?"

"I'm not sure. There is a couple here that want me to go with them. They say it's on your orders."

"It is. You'll be safe. They'll bring you to Cam and me."

"Where are you?"

"I'm out but Cam will be waiting for you at the Galleon."

"Okay, thanks. I'll see you there."

Diane hung up and thanked Jill for her help. She stood and left with her two escorts.

They were at the Galleon twenty minutes later. When they arrived at the third-floor room, one of the guards opened the door to let them in. He didn't look too happy.

Kailey stepped out of the bedroom and saw Diane. Instead of going to her and hugging her as she usually did, she asked angrily, "Have you seen Cam?"

"No. Isn't he here?"

"No, he isn't. I told him not to leave. It's too dangerous out there right now."

I stepped to the open door. The guard gave me a look that could kill.

"Sorry," I said. "Is Kailey back yet?"

"Yes, I'm back," Kailey said from inside the room. "Where have you been?"

I held up a white sack containing a half-dozen chocolate honeybuns.

"Want a donut?" I said.

She gave me a look a lot like the guard did only I could actually see little daggers flying toward me. I looked at Diane. She didn't look too happy either.

"Okay, I couldn't just sit here while that madman is out there getting me into more trouble. I have to find him now."

"I just finished looking at the tapes from the hotel security cameras. I wasn't able to keep them because the CIA was already there. I watched you shoot Bexley in the shoulder, hand Henry the gun, and leave. As soon as you were out the door, Henry shot Bexley in the leg by accident. He didn't know how to handle a gun and it went off. They're blaming that on you too."

I sat on the sofa and leaned back. How much worse could it get? Walter came to me and put his head in my lap. I scratched it subconsciously while I thought about all the evidence they had against me.

"I want all of you to distance yourselves from me. I can't drag you into this. I'll find a way out. I always do."

"Don't be crazy, Cam," Diane said. "I'm going to stay with you until we get this guy and clear your name."

"We're not going anywhere," Kailey said. "It's going to take all of us to get you out of this one."

"Did you see Stan Whittle in any of those tapes?"

"Yes, I did. He was with a girl named Holly Simmons. They do jobs together once in a while. They're not usually this sloppy. My guess is Camata wants you dead but doesn't want Brittany to know he was the one to order the hit. It was a stupid plan. Brit will have him killed as soon as she's released. Bexley, Stan, and Holly were all three there to get to you."

"Well, that's one down and two to go then. I'm going to have to find them before they find me again."

Diane came to the sofa and hugged me. With all the commotion, I hadn't told her welcome home.

"How was your trip?" I asked.

"It was fun, but I wish I wouldn't have gone."

"This was going to happen whether you were here or not. There's nothing you could have done about it."

She hugged me again. "Did you say you had some chocolate rolls?"

As mad as everyone was at me, they managed to eat the rolls. I gave one to each of Diane's escorts. They were eating them on their way out. The last one went to the guard outside the door. He took it even though he still looked mad at me. It was a good thing I ate mine at the bakery.

My cell rang. It was Jack. "Cam, I just noticed something here at the marina. There's a boat sitting here in slip twelve that is identical to Diane's. I looked it over. I could tell the numbers had been covered recently. My guess is someone covered them with new numbers and then peeled them back off. The same on the stern. The name on the back says Overboard Marina, but it had been covered too. The area around all the decals is cleaner than the rest."

"I'm with Diane and Kailey at the Galleon. Can you keep an eye on that boat?"

"I've already set a camera aiming at it. If anyone goes on board it'll signal my phone. I called their marina. They said some guy named Alexander Drake rented it for a week."

"Good job, thanks. I'll put Diane on."

I handed Diane the phone and they talked for a while as Kailey and I stepped onto the balcony.

John Bexley lay in the hospital bed at KWMC. Luckily the shot to his leg was superficial, but his shoulder hurt like hell. There were guards outside the door and his hand was shackled to the bed. *How the hell am I going to get out of here? Derringer has to pay for this.*

Agent in Charge Marlon Hayes from Miami stepped into the room.

"How ya feeling, John?"

"Sore. Someone tried to kill me."

"Yeah, Cam Derringer. Do ya know 'im?"

"We've met."

"Yes, I know. A few months ago, you tried to kill him. Then you two had a shoot-out at Marathon that left five dead."

"I didn't have anything to do with that. I was sitting at a picnic table when he opened up on me."

"Yeah, I saw the tapes. You're in a lot of trouble. If it were up to me, we'd hang you in the town square. But you have friends in high places from your days with the CIA. When you get feeling better, you'll be released."

John smiled at this. "I'll be free to go?"

Marlon nodded. "But I'll be watchin' you. One wrong move and I'll put a bullet in your back."

"That would be murder," John said.

"Yeah," Marlon said and left the room.

John started a burst of uncontrollable laughter that made his shoulder hurt even more.

I watched the crowd below the balcony. Tourists were barhopping. A boat cruised slowly past heading into the marina. A topless girl was waving at everyone from the bow as they passed. Only in Key West. Kailey waved back at her.

The sun was going down and the town would come even more alive in a few minutes. I thought about Stacy being stuck in that jail cell for no reason.

"I'd like for someone to go check on Stacy," I said. "She shouldn't be in jail and alone."

"I agree, but you can't possibly go see her. I'll send someone in the morning."

"She should have a bail hearing tomorrow. I already know there won't be any chance she'll get out. But she has to be set free one way or the other."

"Cam, what are you thinking? It better not be what I think it is."

"Wouldn't you do something to get me out if I were in there?"

"It's too risky. Let me work on it. She's in a local cell, but it's the CIA that has her. They'll be transferring her to Langley in a day or two."

"That's when we can get her," I said.

"You're not thinking straight. I'll talk to Hoffman. He's the assistant director now and he owes me. There's a chance I can get her released into my custody."

"Robert Hoffman?" I asked her.

"Yes, do you know him?"

"Yeah, if it's the same one. We went to Yale together. Does he know I'm the one they're after?"

"More than likely he does. Or he just hasn't put the name together yet."

"Really? How many Cam Derringers do you know who live in Key West?"

"Just let me talk to him. We'll figure something out."

Diane joined us with two drinks. She handed us each one then stepped back inside to get hers. "What's the plan?" she asked when she returned.

"I'm going to talk to the assistant director tomorrow. Maybe I can get Stacy out of jail. It's a long shot, but it's something."

We sat in the porch chairs and sipped our drinks. A plan was starting to form in my head. Now I just needed to sort out the details.

Kailey excused herself. She said she was going to make a call to the police department to check on Stacy.

When she returned, she said, "Stacy is going to be okay."

Chapter 20

"Is there any way you can disguise me?" I asked Kailey.

"Cam, you're six foot four of solid muscle. You tower over every man down there on the street. Do you really think no one would recognize you if your hair was blond?"

"I could bend over a little."

She just shook her head and sipped her drink.

"This is a gay community," Diane said. "I can get you some women's clothing. You'd just be another drag queen."

"I know you're joking, but that just might work," I said seriously.

"You'd really do that?" she asked.

"If it would get me out of here and on the street, I would."

Diane looked at Kailey who shrugged her shoulders. "It would be fun getting him ready," she said.

"What size do you think he'd wear?" Diane asked.

"Huge."

They laughed but now my plan was starting to come together. I might be able to find Stan and Holly while keeping Kailey and Diane out of harm's way.

"If you find yourself out and need a place to crash," I said, "Dave and Wanda are back in the same house they lived in last time. They said we could hide there."

"What brought that up?" Diane asked.

"I just remembered about them. I don't really think this drag thing is going to work out. I figure we're going to need all the safe places we can find."

"Is everything okay, Stacy?" Ryan asked.

He'd been to her cell at least once every hour since she was locked up.

"I'm okay." She was getting anxious, and her claustrophobia was getting the best of her. She had never experienced it before, but now she needed to get out of there.

"Is there any way I can get out of here for a few minutes? Maybe walk around a little?"

Ryan thought about it for a minute. "Let me see what I can do. I'll be right back."

While he was gone Stacy walked around the cell and breathed deeply. She thought about Cam. *I wonder if he's still okay. I hope they don't find him. He'll never prove we're innocent if he's locked up.*

Ryan returned with a female guard. "She's going to walk you around for a few minutes," he said. "This is Kyla Douglas."

"Thanks, Kyla. I just need to get out for a few minutes."

"That's okay, honey. It happens. We have a yard you can stay in for a while."

"Thanks, Kyla," Ryan said then turned to Stacy. "I'll see you when you get back."

Kyla led her to the yard, which was located behind the police station. It had an eight-foot fence with concertina wire looped around the top. The area was only about twenty yards long and ten yards wide, but it was outside under the stars.

Stacy took a deep breath. "Is it okay if I walk around?" she asked.

"Sure, that's why you're out here. Walk the whole perimeter. The best spot is over there in that corner," she said and pointed to a spot as far away from the building as you could get. "We call that freedom point."

"Okay, thank you."

When Stacy started to walk away, Kyla said, "Kailey sent someone for you," then she turned and stepped back inside the building. This would more than likely be her last day on the job, but her debt would be paid and she'd have a better life.

Stacy wondered what she meant by that as she walked the fence line. When she came to freedom point, she saw a car flash its lights in the parking lot. She looked around, but she was the only one there. Then she noticed the gate in front of her was ajar. *Is this a jailbreak?*

We ordered a late supper from Caroline's Café and had it delivered. While we waited the girls planned what kind of clothing I would wear. Diane said she'd go out in a few minutes and pick it up. Things were getting serious now; I was starting to have second thoughts.

As we were talking, Walter jumped up and ran to the door. We stopped and watched him.

"What's up with him?" Diane asked.

"It's probably the food," I said.

The door opened and the guard was standing there filling the doorway. He stepped aside and Stacy walked in.

Stan and Holly walked the streets near the old town. There were so many tourists it was almost impossible for them to see the forest for the trees, so to speak.

"We'll never find him here," Stan said. "Let's go to his boat. He's bound to show up sooner or later."

"He might be there, but I doubt it. The police will have it staked out. No, according to the radio, this is the last place he was spotted."

"Maybe he's in a hotel."

They walked past Sloppy Joe's and were heading for Mallory Square when Holly said, "Let's walk the hotels on the way. We can start at the docks and walk east. Who knows, something might jump out at us. We're not going to find him in a crowd like this."

They turned up Greene Street and walked to Simington Street, turned left, and headed toward the resort area.

The first hotels they came to were the Pier House on the left and the Hyatt on the right.

"Let's start on the right," Holly said. "There are only two hotels here then we'll turn around, come back here, and hit the ones up the street toward Mallory Square."

They entered the grounds and walked around all the buildings.

"What are we even looking for here?" Stan asked.

"Anything that might look out of place."

They came to a bench under a Banyon Tree and sat down. "Let's just watch for a few minutes," Stan said, "and then we'll move to the next one. If he's hiding in the area, we might see him making a move."

Fifteen minutes later, they stood and moved to the next hotel, the Galleon.

"Stacy, how'd you get out of jail?" I asked when I saw her.

"I walked out. I think Kailey might be able to fill you in."

I looked at Kailey. "We had to get her out. I pulled some strings and here she is."

"Is she out legally?"

"Well, that depends on how you look at it. The guard told her where to go. No one told her not to leave."

The TV, which had been playing quietly on the news station in the background, suddenly flashed Stacy's face. The caption below read, "Stacy Monroe, daring jail break."

"I guess that answers my question," I said.

"You know how the news hypes things up," Kailey said.

"Am I an escaped convict now?" Stacy asked.

I looked at Kailey again.

"No, honey, the CIA will release another statement saying that you were released into their custody. I made a call a while ago. The police just haven't gotten the memo yet."

"If that's true, where is the CIA?"

"I'm the CIA, sort of," Kailey said. "I'll make another call."

"What's going to happen to the policewoman who let me go?"

"She going to live a life of luxury in another country."

She excused herself and went to the veranda. I could see her out there on her phone. It looked as if the conversation was getting heated. When she returned, she said, "Everything will be okay."

"And me?" I asked. "Are they still looking for me?"

"I'm afraid they are. They're convinced it was the two of you who pulled this off. They let Stacy go into my custody because they trust me. They know of our relationship though and don't trust that you'll stay around."

"They still think it was Stacy and me who killed those people. That's crazy."

"They don't know you and you saw the movie," Kailey said.

"I have to find a way to prove it wasn't me."

"Didn't anyone see you diving that morning?" Kailey asked.

"I don't think so. We left early and were gone most of the day. We went to a beach afterward, but it was deserted. No one was at the dock when we left or returned."

"That doesn't sound good. This place is packed with tour boats and divers."

"Yeah, we thought it was just lucky that we were alone."

"There was that one boat anchored close by," Stacy said. "Remember, they made another boat turn away from the area."

"Yeah, I remember, but I didn't get a good look at it. It was like they were working in the area and kind of shut it down. They didn't stop us though."

"That was probably set up by Stan," Kailey said. "He didn't want anyone to see you."

Things didn't look good for us. I was going to have to speed up my plan. It was only a matter of time before the police found me. That was if Stan didn't find me first.

Chapter 21

Stan and Holly entered the Galleon parking lot. The office was just ahead on the left. The buildings on the right were set right on the docks. The view from those rooms would be magnificent.

They both leaned back and looked at the buildings. A man was standing on the third floor of one of the buildings smoking a cigarette. He eventually put the cigarette out and field stripped it. It was odd that he didn't return to the room.

"Do you see him?" Stan asked.

"Yeah, it's like he's guarding the room. Military. Did you see the way he tore that cigarette down so there would be no trace?"

"Yeah, let's sit down over there and watch for a while," Stan said, nodding toward an area with two tables and chairs under a shelter. There were two tall ashtrays next to the tables. "It's a smoking area."

They sat and watched the man for a few minutes. Holly pulled out a cigarette and lit it.

"When did you start smoking?" Stan asked.

"When I was eighteen. Only one a day. I thought this was as good a time as any."

The door behind the man opened and a very attractive woman stepped out. She said something to him and then they both looked down at us.

"What do you make of that?" Holly asked.

"I believe we were just introduced to Kailey."

"The assassin that works with Brittany?"

"I believe so. Look away and get ready to leave if he comes this way."

She glanced up at the balcony again. They were still looking at them.

"I think we've been made," Holly said. "Let's get out of here and watch from somewhere else."

They stood and hugged and walked to the entrance. They spoke a few words then each went a separate way, waving goodbye.

Kailey went back inside. "I think Stan and Holly just found us," she said.

"They're here?" I asked.

"They were watching the room from the lot. I'm sure it was them."

"Let's go," I said, picking up my gun.

"We can't go out there shooting. Besides, they're gone now."

"Well, they're as close as they've been. I'm gonna go look for 'em. The rest of you, find a new place to stay."

With that, I opened the door and stepped out.

"Wait," Kailey said. "I'm going with you."

When she came out, she told the guard to get Stacy, Diane, and Walter and move them to another hotel. "Call me when you get there."

Kailey and I ran down the stairs and out of the lot.

"Which way did they go?" I asked.

"She went this way and he went that way," she said, pointing.

"I'll look for him. You go that way. Call if you spot anything."

She took off at a run. I did the same in pursuit of Stan. It only took twenty seconds before I was in a crowd of people walking the streets. He could have gone anywhere.

The good thing was he knew where I was now. The only way I could find him was if he found me first. That might be dangerous, but it was the only way. At least now Stacy would be hidden away from me and him.

I stopped on the corner of Duval and Green Streets. Kailey came up on my left. "Did you see anything?" she asked me but already knew the answer.

"No. It's an easy town to get lost in."

"It's not safe for you out here in the open. We need to get back to the hotel."

"I think I'm going to stay out here for a few minutes. They might still be around."

"I know you, Cam. You're trying to coax them out into the open by being a target. That's a dumb idea. They're cold-blooded murderers."

"Yes they are, but everyone thinks I am. It's what I have to do."

Ten minutes later, walking the street, someone else recognized me. They started calling for the police. I had to run again. This time, once I was out of sight I ducked into the Hard Rock Café. I pulled my hat down to cover my face and went up the steps. I stood out on the balcony and watched the street. When I saw the police car pull up a block away, I faded back into the shadows but kept watching.

"Do you need a drink, Cam?" Kira Popova said from behind me.

She's a Russian girl who moved to Key West three years ago. I helped her get her citizenship. She's a waitress here at the Hard Rock now.

"I could use a glass of water, Kira. Thanks."

"If the police come this way, I can hide you. Don't worry."

I nodded at her and she left. I was still watching the action on the street a couple of minutes later when she returned with my water and a Wild Turkey and Coke.

I took both and sat down. I called Kailey and told her where I was. She was still on the street near the police cars.

"I think they're getting ready to leave. Someone else called at the same time and said they spotted you and Stacy four blocks away. Any bets on who that was they spotted?"

"You know, that could come in handy. If we see them again, we could call the police and say we spotted Cam and Stacy. When they see how much they look like us, they might have second thoughts and at least question them."

"I'll see you back at the hotel in an hour," Kailey said. "I'll walk over to where they were spotted. It was on the other side of Fat Tuesdays."

I thought this would be a good chance to start my plan.

"Okay, see ya there."

When we hung up, I drank down my Wild Turkey and then took a slug of water. I went through my contacts and brought up a name I entered three months ago.

"Who is this? How did you get this number?" Camata asked when he answered his private cell number.

"It's me, Cam Derringer, and I got the number from you. Remember?"

Silence, then, "What do you want?"

"You, now. I was going to forget about you, but now you've made it personal. Stan and Holly told me you hired them to kill me. That was right before I put a bullet in each of them. I'll have to wait to finish off John Bexley. The CIA has him right now. And there's the matter of Brittany. She is pissed. I'm glad I'm not you, but she promised me first crack at ya."

"I don't know what you're talking about. I didn't hire anyone to kill you."

"Well, she's on her way to Bermuda now. She said she would hold you until I arrived."

"No, please. It wasn't me. You have the wrong man."

"I've been telling everyone that myself since you set me up. No one believes me either."

"Where are you? I'll send someone to help you get away," he said.

"All I'm going to tell you is that I'll be in Big Pine Key tomorrow. I want you to come here. I want you to tell the police the truth."

Silence again for a few seconds. "I'll be in Big Pine Key tomorrow afternoon. I'll call this number when I get there. But you have to stop Brittany."

"I'll try. She's already in the air though. You had better hide until tomorrow."

I hung up the phone. *If this works like I hope it will, Camata will check with Stan first and find out he's alive. Then he'll tell them I'll be in Big Pine Key tomorrow. I know the area well. I think I can set a trap for them.*

I stayed on the side streets and returned to the hotel. The guard had taken the girls and Walter and left. I was there alone waiting for Kailey, I thought.

I went into the bedroom on my way to the shower. Naked Kailey was lying on the bed.

"Girl, do you have no shame?" I asked.

"Why don't you come here and shame me?"

"Give me two minutes," I said and headed for the shower.

Thirty seconds later, the shower door opened and Kailey stepped in. "I couldn't wait that long," she whispered softly into my neck.

I held her and thought how bad it would be if I never got to do this again. There was no way I was going to let them lock me up forever.

Fifteen minutes later, we were lying on the shower floor. The warm water was running over us. We were breathing hard but still moving together. Finally spent, we lay on the warm floor and held each other.

"I love you," I said.

"I know. Remember, I told you that you would the first time we met."

"Yeah, I was a little slow at getting the memo."

"I love you too, Cam. One day I plan on marrying you."

"Do you think you'll ever be able to? Justice and all."

"Someday I think Malinda will be over Justice. She already told me that if she was, she would let me out."

"So, Malinda will never get out?"

"I don't think she can. She's too informed. The government wouldn't take the chance."

"It's hard to believe that our government has its own hit squad."

She reached down and held me. "What have we here?"

"I'm ready if you are," I said.

"I'm always ready."

"Can we move it to the bed?"

"I insist."

Stan looked at his phone and saw Camata's name. "Shit, it's him again."

"Answer it," Holly said. "Maybe he's changed his mind."

"I *thought* you were still alive," Camata said.

"Why wouldn't I be?"

"Cam called me a few minutes ago. He said he shot the two of you."

Stan laughed. "He has quite the imagination. We did find him though, but Kailey spotted us, so we got out of there."

"Kailey saw you?" he yelled.

"Calm down. They can't find us."

"You've got one more chance. Cam wants me to meet him in Big Pine Key tomorrow afternoon. I want you two to go there tonight and get a room. He'll be looking for you tomorrow as he's coming to meet with me. Just kill him. Brittany is on her way here. She wants a piece of me too. I'm going to set a trap for her and get rid of her once and for all."

"So I take it you won't be here tomorrow."

"Of course not. I'm not going to walk into a trap."

"But you want us to?"

"No, I want you to *set* a trap."

"The fifty thousand from today is back on the table or I'll just leave with what I have and you can take care of all of them yourself."

"Just get it done. You'll be paid," Camata spat and hung up.

Stan chuckled. "What a dumb ass."

Chapter 22

John Bexley dressed with the help of his nurse and waited for his discharge papers. "Tell that doctor to hurry up," he said. "I have things I need to do."

His papers arrived ten minutes later. John took them, folded them up and stuck them in his back pocket. He hurried out of the hospital. His first task was going to be finding Cam Derringer. Hopefully, he'd find Holly at the same time. That dirty little bitch set him up.

"You did what?" Brittany yelled. "You know he's going to find Cam and kill him."

"We had to let him go. Orders from upstairs," Agent Marcello Lombardi said.

"How could they let him go when he tried to kill Cam two months ago?"

"We don't have any proof it was him who shot Cam. No witnesses, no one saw him in the area."

"I did and I told them that."

"Sorry Brit. My hands are tied."

"I have to get out of here," she said.

"That's the good news. You'll be released tomorrow."

"Today. I have to get out today."

"We can't do that. We have a tail on Bexley and if we let you out, you'll spoil the whole thing. We know how you are. You'll go in shooting and ask questions later."

Marcello left the room. Malinda sat on her bed and made a plan for tomorrow.

My phone rang. It was Diane. She said they were at the Tropicana Inn on Duval Street.

"Stay put. We'll be there sometime this evening."

"Why is Walter acting so funny?"

"What's he doing?"

"Well, he was in the other room by himself. When I walked in, he was sitting up, but as soon as he saw me, he fell over backward."

"Oh, that. It's his new trick. Did Stacy see it?"

"No."

"She doesn't believe he knows how to sit up."

"I don't think he does."

"He does, but only for me."

"Whatever. I'll see you in a while."

Kailey and I decided to take a ride around Key West. I told her I wanted to go to Garrison Bight to see the boat Jack was talking about. We found Jack on his laptop. He was scanning all the surveillance cameras in Key West.

"I might get lucky and spot one of them," he said as he stood to hug Kailey. As usual, the hug lasted too long.

"I'm gonna check out the boat," I said.

"It's down at the end of the dock."

Kailey walked with me to the boat.

"It's identical to Diane's," I said. "And I see what Jack means about the numbers. They do look as if they were taped over recently."

Kailey jumped down into the boat. She looked under the seats and around the cockpit.

"It's empty. When they left it, they took everything with them," she said.

"Yeah, they're probably not planning on coming back."

I thought about meeting them the next day at Big Pine Key. They would be wise to take the boat and a car if they were going to try to ambush me. They might just be back.

We returned to Jack's boat where he was still looking through the cams.

"What do ya think?" he asked.

"I think you're right. That could very easily have been the boat that was used in the attack. I don't think they'll be back for it though. It's cleaned out," Kailey said.

"Jack, can I borrow your skiff?" I asked.

"Sure, where ya goin'? Do you need some help?"

"I'm going to my boat. I know the police have it staked out. I'll drop anchor in the bay and scuba in. It's getting dark now. I'll be able to get in and out, no problem."

"I'm going too then," Kailey said.

"No. One person might be able to get in and out, but two would probably draw attention."

"Why would you want to go to your boat?" she asked.

"For one thing, I don't have my medicine. The doc told me to take it all. Then I want to see how much damage they did to it when they searched it. I don't like people going through my things."

"I could just walk right up there and get your medicine and check your boat," Jack said. "They're not looking for me."

"If they find you with the medicine, they'll know you're bringing it to me. I'll be okay."

"Okay then. The tanks are in the dock locker and the keys are in the boat. Help yourself."

"Thank you."

Kailey pulled her phone out of her pocket and looked at it.

"Shit," she said. "Bexley is alive and was just released from the hospital."

"Who told you?"

"Marcello, a friend, just sent me a text."

We all took an automatic look around the docks and the lot entrance.

"We'll keep a lookout for 'im," I said.

"Now you have two different people wanting you dead and the police wanting you in jail," Kailey said. "Do you really think it's a good idea to go to your boat?"

"It's something I have to do," I said.

"I don't know what you're up to, but I don't like it."

"I'll be fine."

Kailey gave me one of those looks. I knew she didn't trust me and with good reason. I wasn't going to go to my boat. I was going to Big Pine Key. But I wanted to go alone and by water.

"Call me as soon as you get back," she said.

"I will."

"I'm going to the Tropicana Inn to check on the girls. I want you to stay there with us tonight."

"What about your boat?" I asked. "Do you think the police are watching it?"

"That depends on who's working and how good of friends you have. A few of them know you spend a lot of time on it. If they haven't said anything, it would be safe. But, on the other hand, if one of them wanted to get a promotion..."

I thought about who knew I used to live on that boat and which of them would turn me in. It was a short list, but it was a list.

"Yeah, let's don't take that chance," I said.

"Alright, I'll see ya tonight. Be careful at whatever it is you're going to do."

She kissed me and left.

"Are you sure you don't need any help?" Jack asked me when we were alone.

I thought about it for a minute. "Would you mind driving to Big Pine Key in the morning? Don't tell anyone where I am and come armed."

"What's going on, Cam?"

"I made arrangements to meet Camata there around noon. I know he won't come, but I'm sure Stan and Holly will be there. I can set a trap for them."

"And what about Bexley? He's out now."

"I have a feeling he'll be there too."

"You don't want to call the cops and let them handle it?"

"You know as well as I do their hands would be tied. I don't want them to get away this time."

"I don't like it Cam, but you can count me in. Are you going by boat tonight?"

"That's the plan," I said.

"Let me get you some guns. You can't go hunting with a nine-millimeter."

After filling the boat with an assortment of automatic rifles and pistols, I loaded a cooler of water and food and told Jack to call me in the morning when he got close.

"I would not want to be you when Kailey catches up with ya," he said.

"Neither would I."

"Here's a duffel bag for the guns," he said and tossed his old military bag into the boat.

"Thanks, see ya tomorrow. Big Pine Key Resort, B five."

John Bexley watched from the parking lot. His plan was to follow Cam out and shoot him that night. Then Cam got into a boat and idled out of the marina. "Crap. I'll just keep an eye on Jack."

Chapter 23

At midnight, Stan and Holly pulled into the lot at Garrison Bight. Stan wasted no time jumping into the rented skiff they had used in the massacre and firing up the engine.

"I'll see you in Big Pine Key," he told Holly. "Meet me at the Old Wooden Bridge guest house. We have cabin six. I'll be there when I get there."

He pulled out of the Bight and into the dark waters of the gulf. Now he had to depend solely on the GPS and his paper charts to find his way. The number one rule of the water is never to travel unfamiliar waters at night.

Stan knew his trip would take two hours in the daylight even though it was only twenty-four nautical miles. Now he was adding at least fifty percent to that time because he was going to go a mile out instead of trying to navigate the reefs and humps. In the daylight, he could get through by watching the changing colors of the water, but now there was no color. It was going to be a long night.

The next morning, Jack came to the docks early to organize the fishing tours. By five o'clock, he was finished. That was when he noticed that the skiff was gone. He checked the camera and clearly saw Stan set out in the skiff. He called Cam. Cam.

"It looks like Stan left with the skiff last night," he said.

"If he made it through the channels, he might be here now. I'm at the resort. Can you come this morning?"

"I can be there in about an hour," Jack said.

"Perfect, room B five."

Jack packed a bag and threw it in the back of his truck. He pulled out of the lot and headed north to Big Pine. That time of the morning it would only take about a half-hour.

Bexley watched Jack pack and leave. He stayed a half-mile back and followed him. *He's in a hurry to get somewhere today.*

It bothered him that Stan and Holly weren't around. Had they been called off? *I doubt it. I have a feeling I'll be running into them. They probably think I'm dead or in jail. That will definitely work to my advantage.*

There were three cars between Jack and John when Jack turned on his signal and turned right onto Long Beach Drive. By the time John turned, Jack was already pulling into Big Pine Key Resort.

Bexley didn't slow down and barely looked Jack's way. He'd have time to find his truck when he returned. *My guess is I just found Cam.*

When Holly woke that morning, Stan was sleeping in a recliner in the corner. She went to the office and got two coffees and four fresh donuts. When she returned, Stan was coming out of the shower.

"Did I wake you?" she asked. "Got ya goodies."

"Thanks. I need them. I had a hell of a night. Even a mile out I bumped the bottom. I had to stop and read the charts. I hit the only bad spot for a quarter mile. Luckily, I didn't get stuck. I backed away, turned starboard, and idled away for five minutes."

"I still don't know why you wanted to bring the boat. We should be able to get away in the car."

"Let's hope we can, but if not, we have a backup."

"How are we going to find Cam?" she asked then took a bite of her donut.

She had to wait for him to swallow a mouthful of his donut and then take a sip of coffee. "He'll call Camata to let him know where to be. Camata will call me."

"Do you really think it's going to be that simple?"

"Nope, no way. Cam's already got an ambush set up for us. He knows Camata won't come. He figures we'll be there though."

"What about Bexley?"

"Hopefully, he's dead."

"So, are we going to wait here all day for the call?" she asked while stuffing the last bite into her mouth.

"No, I thought we'd go out and explore the Key. We need to know every nook and cranny, at least the best we can. We can take the car first then come back here and get the boat. We're sitting on Spanish Harbor Channel. It'll make a good escape route to either the Gulf or the Atlantic."

"That sounds good. We should be able to get out one way or the other."

"Hey Jack, thanks for coming," I said when I opened the door.

"Not a problem. I'm glad we have a boat and a car here. Do you think *they* do?"

"Were there any cars left in the lot this morning?"

Jack thought a minute. "No, I don't remember any. There was one car that drove through, but they circled and went to the top of the drive. I think they were waiting for someone."

"Then yes, I think they have a car with 'em too. They're pros. They aren't going to get trapped in here."

"And I guess you have one of your masterplans?"

"Yep."

"Care to share?"

"We're going to tell them to meet us down here on Long Beach. They have to either drive or boat right past us. Then we follow them in and they're trapped. One way in, one way out."

"That's your big plan? Making someone have to shoot their way out to get past us."

"Well, yeah. I haven't worked out the details yet, but you've got the basic idea."

Jack shook his head and said, "I should have known better."

"Look at it this way, we'll know where they are. Right now we have to keep looking over our shoulders."

"You're right about that part. They'll be right in front of us, shooting at us."

There was a knock on my door. I picked my gun up off the table and moved to the door. Jack stood behind it.

"Who is it?" I asked.

"Kailey!" she screamed.

I looked at Jack. "Did you tell her?"

He shook his head.

More pounding on the door.

"I think you had better let her in," Jack said. "She's getting mad."

I lowered my gun and unlocked the door. Kailey walked in with a look on her face that could have killed.

I held my hands up and said, "I was only trying to protect you."

"How, by killing the only man I ever loved?"

"If you're talking about me, I'll be okay. Jack is here to help me."

She looked at Jack. "Abbott and Costello. You two together are a danger to yourselves."

"I'm going to let that comment go because I know you don't mean it. We work quite well together. I believe I came through the door a few months ago just in time to save your life."

"Yeah, and twenty minutes later, I was watching them load you into an ambulance."

I just stared at her. She put her arm around me and kissed me. Then she turned to Jack. "I didn't mean that about you." Then she kissed him.

"Am I Abbott or Costello?" I asked.

She smiled. "What's the plan?"

"Oh, you're going to love this," Jack said.

"We're going to trap them down the road here and shoot 'em," I said, giving her the short version.

She looked at me and didn't say anything.

"Okay, what would you do?" I asked.

"I'd have one of us already in there with a sniper rifle. One of us here to follow them in and one in the boat in case they come in that way."

"That's what I said."

"Okay, what if Bexley shows up?"

"That's the uncertainty in the plan. We may have to cover our backs too."

"You're talking a possible crossfire."

"Possibly," I said. "How did you know where to find us?" I asked her.

"I followed Jack. One car back. He didn't even look for a tail."

"I did too," he said. "You're just good."

"Let's get something to eat while we wait for Malinda," Kailey said.

Chapter 24

"Okay you guys," Brittany said. "It's tomorrow. Let me out of here."

"We're working on it," Marcello said. "Bexley has left town. We have a trace on him, but you'll never find him."

"Did he go north or south?"

"He can only go north from here," Marcello said.

"How long ago did he leave?"

"Sorry Brit, can't tell ya. And did you know that Stacy Monroe walked out of jail yesterday?"

"She was released?"

"Not exactly. A guard let her into the yard and the gate wasn't locked. Kailey called and said she was in her custody. There was so much going on that we agreed to it."

"She's innocent anyway. If you knew her you'd know that."

Forty-five minutes later, Brittany left the base. She was picked up by her bodyguard at the front gate.

She called Kailey. "Where are you?"

"Big Pine Key Resort."

"Is Bexley there?"

"We don't know but we think Stan and Holly are."

"My guess is Bexley is there too. The CIA released him but they have a tracker on 'im somehow. How did you get Stan and Holly there?"

"Cam called Camata and told him to meet him here around noon. He said you were on the way to Bermuda to kill him."

"And you know Camata won't come but he'll send them."

"Right."

"Then I'll have to go to Bermuda and kill him, I guess," Brittany said.

"I'll go with you. This is all because of him."

"Where are Stacy and Diane?" Malinda asked.

"I left them in the Tropicana Inn. Would you go and check on them?"

"I will and then I'll be there in about an hour."

"See ya then," Kailey said as they hung up.

Bexley pulled his hat down and walked into the resort. The roads inside ran large circles around the cottages. It didn't take him long to spot Jack's truck. There were two more cars parked in front of the same cottage.

He walked toward the cottage keeping one hand on his gun. The front door was standing open. He could see a man and woman inside talking. *That sure looks like Cam and Kailey.*

This was a little unsettling. *Cam is dangerous enough and so is Jack, but now Kailey is with them. That's not good.*

He wondered what they were all doing there. *Is this just where Cam is hiding?*

He quickly turned and walked away when he saw them step out the door. Once out of sight, he hurried to the side of the next cottage to hide.

They got in the truck and pulled away. Instead of following them, he decided to investigate the inside of the room.

The door was locked but picked easily. The inside of the cottage was cleaner and more comfortable than he'd thought it would be.

It was sitting right on the water and, more than likely, one of the boats at the dock belonged to Cam.

He picked up a few papers and turned them over. Nothing was interesting or helpful. He looked under the bed. Nothing there either. When he opened the closet, though, he saw a duffel. He opened it to see the amount of weaponry they had with them. *They're planning on a big battle.*

He closed it up and left the room. He thought about going back into the room and waiting for them, but with three of them, he might not have a chance. *No, I'll pick 'em off one at a time.*

We were sitting in the Florida Keys Café eating bacon and eggs when a black SUV pulled into the lot. I watched them inside their car looking at their computer screen. They didn't seem to be coming in here, they were more interested in something down the road toward the resort.

They sat for a minute then pulled back out and drove north on Highway One.

"CIA," Kailey said. "Malinda said they were tracking Bexley. He must be close."

"Do you think he followed me too?" Jack asked.

"Probably so," Kailey said. "We led him right here."

"That's a good thing," I said. "We wanted them all in one place. But now we have to work around the CIA. They're probably following him to find me."

"Probably. We need to get you hidden. We're sitting ducks out here."

The waitress came to the table. "Do you need anything else?" she asked.

Just then a sheriff's car pulled into the lot. I looked that way. They seemed to be in a hurry.

"Shit," I said.

The waitress looked out the window and then at me. "Come on, Cam. You can go through the kitchen and out the back door."

I didn't think she would remember who I was. I hadn't been there for a few years.

"Thanks, Maggie," I said and stood. I read the name on a tag from her blouse. She was better at remembering than I was.

"We'll pick you up around back in a few minutes," Kailey said.

I left just as the deputies walked into the restaurant. Ten minutes later, Jack pulled to the rear parking lot and I got in his truck.

"How'd it go inside?" I asked.

"They recognized me," Jack said. "They're doing a sweep of the area. I guess the CIA gave them a heads-up that you might be around here because Bexley is. One of them remembered me from the shooting here a few years ago. They knew we were friends. I told them that I was here on a date. They didn't believe me, but what could they do?"

I lay down in the back seat in case they were watching Jack. "Let's get back to the resort and get our guns," I said. "I think we need to get out of the area."

"We'll use Jack's boat," Kailey said. "They won't be looking for that one."

As we turned onto Long Beach Road, we saw another black SUV coming toward us from the beach end. They were swarming around us like bees.

John Bexley sat in his rental car in the crowded parking area for the RV park and watched as the CIA and sheriff cars rolled past. *They have a*

tracker on me. He looked around the lot for a car that looked as if had been there a while. He found just what he wanted. It was a blue Ranger that looked to be about twenty years old. The windows were covered with thick dust. He knew how to hot wire that one.

He pulled into the empty spot beside it and got out. After forcing down the window on the truck, he reached inside and unlocked the door. No alarm. In less than a minute, the truck came to life.

He opened the trunk of his rental and pulled out his two handguns. Now he wished he would have taken one of the rifles from the duffel inside the room.

The truck smelled of stale cigars and beer as he drove out of the RV area and up A1A.

Malinda pulled up in front of cottage B five just as Kailey came out the door with a backpack.

"What's up?" Malinda asked.

"Cam and Jack are going into the channel in Jack's skiff. There are too many police and CIA around here."

"If you guys spotted them, then I'm sure John did too. I knew they'd fuck this thing up when they told me they were tracking him. What's the plan for us?"

"We'll take my car and watch the road after Camata calls Cam." She looked at her watch. "That'll be a few more hours."

Jack and I walked out the door just then and heard the girls' conversation. I was carrying the duffel.

"We're loading the boat," I said. "We'll be in the channel."

"Yeah, Kailey told me. Be careful out there. There's nowhere to hide."

"I'm gonna get the poles from my truck. At least we can look like we're fishing," Jack said.

"Do you have any idea where Stan and Holly are?" Malinda asked.

"No, but I'm sure they're on the Key somewhere."

"We're going to drive around the area. We might get lucky and spot 'em."

"We'll call as soon as we hear from Camata," Jack said. "Let's get out of here."

We loaded our guns and poles into the boat and pushed off. Once we were in the channel, we turned to port and headed toward Big Pine and Bella's Sandbar.

Chapter 25

Stan and Holly returned to the marina after exploring the key. It was rather simple to navigate Big Pine Key. They were on State Road 4A. They followed it to Key Deer Blvd and took it to A1A. There were side roads that led to other points around the key.

"Let's get into position," Holly said.

"I'll get the boat ready. When I leave the dock, you drive the car south to a central point and wait for my call. When Camata calls me, I'll let you know where to go. If it ends up inland, I'll ditch the boat at BGS South Fishing and walk to Brewers Tiki Bar. You can pick me up there."

"And if it's by water?" she asked.

"I'll let you know. It'll be handy to have a backup on land."

Stan hid his rifle under the bow seat and placed his pistol near the captain's chair while Holly packed him a few previsions. Water, a sandwich and some chips. Then she went to the dock store and bought him a fishing pole and tackle.

Stan kissed her goodbye. "Tomorrow, this will just be a memory," he told her. "We'll spend a day or two in Miami and relax."

"I'm not going to let you relax. You owe me."

"It'll be my pleasure."

Diane's phone rang.

"Hi Diane, it's Ryan Chase."

Diane looked at Stacy and mouthed, "Ryan." Stacy shook her head. "How are you, Ryan?"

"I think you know. Have you seen Stacy?"

"I saw her yesterday. She said she was set free."

"That she was, only it was a mistake. We need her to come back here now."

"What about the CIA? Wasn't she set free by them? I believe she is in the care of Kailey Arlington."

"That doesn't mean anything to us. We didn't set her free."

"Oh, but I believe you did. Did you ask the guard that let her go?"

"We haven't seen her. She disappeared shortly after that."

Diane knew they would never see her again. She had a new life in a new town or country somewhere.

"Well, I'm sorry I can't help you. Maybe she went back home to see her parents."

"Tell her there's an APB on her. She really would be better off coming in on her own."

"You think she's guilty, don't you?"

"No, I don't. But the longer she's on the run the guiltier she looks."

"She's not on the run, Ryan. She was turned over to the CIA. You'll have to live with that. Don't you have some speeders to get or something? You're wasting your time here. And if you do manage to find her, you'll have to deal with the CIA."

"Just please tell her for her own good to call me and I'll come to pick her up. I can make it easy on her."

"If I see her, I'll tell her. Goodbye, Ryan."

"One more thing. We know it was your boat in the shooting. We need to talk to you too."

"It wasn't my boat and I was in the Hamptons when this took place."

Diane hung up before he could argue his case any further. She took the battery out of her phone and put it in her purse.

"They're looking for you and me," she told Stacy.

"I can't believe the mess we're in."

"Our pictures are bound to come up on the TV again. People will recognize us."

"Not too many people in Key West watch TV. Maybe we'll slide on it."

"I wouldn't be too sure. At least I know the owners here. They'll warn me if anyone comes around."

"I wonder who's taking care of Hank."

"I forgot to tell you, Barbie flew back in yesterday. She's at the boat and has him. She called me this morning while you were still asleep."

"That's a relief. I was worried about him."

"I'm sure he's living the good life."

"Yeah."

"Are you okay, Stacy?"

She started to cry. Diane wrapped her arms around her.

"It's all my fault," Stacy said between sobs.

"No, it isn't your fault. You had nothing to do with it."

"If he hadn't taken me diving, he would have an alibi. No one knew we were even out there."

"Cam will be alright. He wouldn't want you to feel bad about this. This is Bexley's and Camata's fault."

Stacy nodded and wiped her eyes. "I've got to do something for him."

"You are. You're staying out of sight so he doesn't have to worry about you."

"We can't stay here forever. Don't you think we should find another place to hide? Maybe somewhere they have already looked."

"We're good here for a while. Just sit tight until we hear from him."

Stacy calmed down some, but Diane was worried about what she might do. She was going to have to keep an eye on her.

"Is it okay if I call Barbie?" Stacy asked.

"I guess it wouldn't hurt. I'll put the battery back in the phone for just a minute."

"Hey, Stacy," Barbie said. "What the hell is going on?"

"It's a long story. I'll fill you in tomorrow when I come home."

"The news said that you and Cam shot up the beach at Marathon and killed a few people."

"It's not true. We're working on it."

"I didn't think it was."

"Is Hank okay?"

"He's fine, but I think he misses you."

"Tell him I'm okay and I'll see him tomorrow."

"Will do. Hey, this is a fancy camera you've got here."

"It's for diving. Cam took me several times. He taught me how to dive."

"Cool."

Diane motioned to Stacy to hang up the phone.

"Okay, Barbie, I've got to go. Hopefully, I'll see you tomorrow."

They hung up and Diane removed the battery again.

"Did you get a trace?" Ryan asked the communications officer.

"We got it. It looks like it came from the eight hundred block of Duval Street. It's closest to the Tropicana Inn."

"Let's go," Ryan said.

He and his partner Joesph Conners left the office and jumped into their squad car. It was only a five-minute drive to the inn but it took twelve because of the traffic.

Angela Sweeny was working the front desk. She saw the police car stop suddenly in front of the office.

"Marsha!" she called.

A teenage girl came to the office. "Go tell Diane to give you her phone. I think it's been tracked. Then I want you to go out the back way and keep running until you're at least five blocks from here."

"Yes, ma'am," Marsha said.

She ran up the steps and banged on Diane's door.

"Who is it?"

"It's Marsha. Let me in."

Diane opened the door and allowed her in.

"Momma said for me to take your phone and run away with it. The police are outside."

"We must have been traced," Stacy said.

Diane got her phone out and handed it to Marsha. Then she handed her the battery.

"Do you know how to put the battery in?" Diane asked her.

"Yep, do it all the time."

"Okay, thanks. Now get going and call someone when you get away from here."

"Don't worry," she said as she ran down the steps and out the back door.

Ryan opened the front door and stepped into the lobby.

"Hey, Angela," he said.

"Hiya, Ryan. How are ya?"

"Doing okay," he said, scratching his head. "You haven't seen Diane Dade around, have you? I need to talk to her."

"Diane? Yes, she was here a few minutes ago. You just missed her."

"Will she be coming back?"

"Probably not today. She just dropped in to say, 'Hi.'"

"Do you mind if I have a look around the hotel?"

"What do you want with her?"

"I only want to talk to her. That's all."

"Why don't you call her?"

"I'd rather talk to her in person. Are you sure she isn't here?"

Just then Ryan's phone rang. He talked for a few seconds and hung up. He turned to Joseph and said, "We just got a new signal from the Monkey Bar on Simington Street, it's only a few blocks. Let's go."

They ran out the door, got in the car, and sped away as fast as they could in bumper-to-bumper traffic.

Angela smiled to herself. She went up the stairs and told Diane they were gone.

"I'm afraid you might have to find another place to stay though."

"We will. Thanks for whatever you did down there."

"You can thank Marsha the next time you see her."

"We will."

Diane and Stacy put Walter on a leash, grabbed their packs, and left the hotel, going out the back way past the pool.

Chapter 26

Jack and I were fishing off Bella's Sandbar. We had drifted along the Spanish Harbor Channel and actually caught a few fish, which we released as fast as we could. My cell rang. I looked down at it and saw Camata's name appear.

"Yes," I said, answering.

"I am in Marathon. Where do you want to meet?"

"Big Pine Key. Long Beach Southeast Point in one hour."

"I have done as you said. I will be alone and I expect you to be also."

"That's the plan. I'll see you there," I said.

"How do I know you won't kill me?"

"I need for you to tell the police everything. We'll set it up so you can get away. I'll have one cop that you can give your statement to."

"Okay, I'll see you there."

After we hung up, I called Kailey. "Camata just called and said he was in Marathon. I think we know he isn't, but he'll be calling Stan shortly and telling him where to meet us."

"We'll be at Long Beach Southeast Point. We can hide the car in the scrubs."

"Jack and I will come in by boat."

"Be careful. You'll be in the open on the water."

"We'll see you see in about twenty-five minutes."

Camata called Stan and told him Cam would be at Long Beach in one hour. "This is your last chance. If he gets away this time, I'll send someone to kill *you*," Camata barked.

"Don't you worry about that. This time I'm not going to try to set him up with some crazy story. This time I'll shoot to kill."

"Call me when it's done."

Stan called Holly and told her to be at the beach as soon as she could get there. "Drop your car somewhere and walk in. I'll be coming on the water in around fifteen minutes."

"Got it. I'm only ten minutes away. Good luck."

"You too."

We were up close to the top of the key near the Old Wooden Bridge. I spun the boat around and started back down toward the beach. As I did I saw a boat screaming south along the shore. It was a match for Diane's boat and the driver was a big man, like me.

"I think that's Stan," I said.

Jack looked at the boat and then pulled his binoculars out of his pack. He held them on the boat for a minute then said, "You're right. That is him. I guess Camata called him as soon as we hung up."

"We'll stay out here in the center and run along with him. I'm gonna call Kailey and give her a heads-up."

Bexley returned to the Big Pine Resort and parked where he could see the entrance without being seen himself. He knew Cam had to come back sooner or later and this was the only place he knew to look.

It was a slightly cloudy day and a chance for thunderstorms. The road to the beach was empty.

He watched an approaching car, but it didn't turn into the resort. As it passed he got a good look at the driver. *Holly.*

He already knew the beach road was a dead end so he waited to see who else came this way. Something was about to go down.

Another car came two minutes later. He ducked down in the seat and watched over the dashboard. *Damn, that looks like Kailey and Brittany.*

He might not have to kill anyone. The party must be about to start. He waited five more minutes hoping Cam and Stan would pass by. When they didn't, he started the old truck and slowly drove down the road toward the beach.

We watched Stan as he kept close to the shore heading to the bottom of Big Pine Key. He followed the shoreline to the right toward Long Beach. We stayed in the channel but didn't lose sight of him. As he got to the bottom of the key and turned he slowed and then stopped his boat. We did the same and both grabbed our fishing rods.

"Stay out here until we see him move toward the beach," I said.

"Let's get our rifles ready, we're going to need them as soon as we get there," Jack said.

"I think we should split up," Stacy said. "They'll be looking for two blonde-haired girls."

"That's probably a good idea. Remember, no matter what Ryan says, you're out of jail legally. The CIA has charge of you now, aka Kailey."

"Yeah, I know, but it hurts to think Ryan is the one who wants me back in jail so badly."

"He's just doing what he thinks is best for you."

"Do you want me to keep Walter?" Stacy asked.

"No, I think I'll take him to Dave. He used to own him anyway. Cam said they're back in the same house they lived in last time they were here."

"Good, he'll be in good hands."

"Wait here a minute," Diane said.

She stepped into the CVS store and bought two burner phones. She came back out and handed one to Stacy. "We'll use these to communicate. There's no way to track 'em."

The two girls swapped numbers. "I'm going to text Cam," Diane said. "I'll give him our numbers."

"That's a good idea. If it rings, I'll know it's one of you."

"Where will you go?" Diane asked.

"I was dating a guy a few weeks ago. He's a good guy. I think he'll let me crash at his place."

"Call him first and feel him out. The news is painting you as a murderer. Some people will jump to the conclusion that you really are."

My phone buzzed on the dash of the boat. I picked it up and read the message.

"Diane and Stacy are splitting up," I told Jack. "Diane is going to Dave's and Stacy to the guy she was dating last month. I've got their new numbers."

"Put 'em in your contacts and erase that message in case we get caught."

"Good idea."

We watched the boat sitting a quarter mile from the East Point. "He's waiting for the right time to attack me when I arrive on the beach."

"I hope Kailey and Malinda are in position."

My phone buzzed again. This time it was Kailey texting me. I relayed the message to Jack again.

"They're hiding off the road. Holly is there, but they haven't spotted her yet."

I told her that Stan was in a boat just off the shore. We were watching him.

There were only five minutes left until we were supposed to meet. "Get ready," I said. "Something is about to go down."

Just then we heard a gunshot. Stan's bow raised and he sped forward toward the beach.

Jack pushed the throttle forward and we raced after him. We heard two more shots just as Stan's boat hit the sandy beach. When he shut his boat off, he must have been able to hear ours because he turned and looked right at us.

We were speeding straight for him. He reached down in his boat and came up with a rifle, aimed quickly, and fired. The bullet ricocheted off the bow. Jack turned to port and then starboard making us a harder target to hit. I fired two quick shots toward Stan with my nine-millimeter.

We heard more shots coming from somewhere on land. The girls had evidently found Holly. I said a quick prayer for their safety.

Stan jumped out of his boat and used it for a shield. I saw him lay his rifle on the gunwale and take aim.

"Turn!" I called.

Jack turned just in time as the bullet slammed into his port side. He circled and came back at Stan again. I raised my gun and emptied it at him. I could see fiberglass splintering on the bow of his boat. Stan dropped down behind the boat for protection.

I slammed another magazine into the nine and dove off the boat into the water as Jack made a closer pass at the beach.

I didn't come up for a breath until I felt the bottom rising.

I took a quick breath and got my bearings. I was only fifteen feet from his boat and straight astern. He couldn't see me. When I looked back at Jack, I could see him taking aim at Stan's boat with his rifle.

I heard two shots from Stan and saw Jack duck down.

John Bexley heard the gunshots as he drove toward the beach. He pulled onto a dirt road that led to Long Beach Trail. He parked his truck on the shoulder and jumped out running toward the noise. He stayed hidden in the shrubs that lined the road. There was swampy water on both sides of the dirt road he was following.

He saw two cars slightly hidden on a small trail. They were the two that had passed him a few minutes ago. He knew that Holly was in a gunfight with Kailey and Brittany.

He decided he wouldn't get into the fight until one side had won. Then he heard more gunshots coming from the left toward the beach.

He stood tall looking through the shrubs. He could see a boat on the water and a man inside firing a rifle toward the beach. He recognized him as Jack, Cam's friend.

This just keeps getting better.

As he moved forward he could tell he was close to one of the shooters. He knelt down and waited. A minute later, he heard footsteps. Someone was running his way.

He sank back further into the bushes and waited. Ten seconds later, he saw Holly running up the trail. When she was beside him, he called to her, "Holly!"

Startled, she jumped sideways and looked his way. His gun was pointing at her. He could tell by the look on her face she knew she didn't have a chance.

He fired his gun, hitting her in the chest. She went down and tried to get back up. He fired again. This time she lay still.

Bexley smiled to himself and sank further back into the cover of the bushes.

I moved toward the boat staying down with only my head above water. I was shallow enough to use my feet to propel me forward.

I heard two more gunshots come from further back on the beach road. Then I heard Jack fire from the boat again. He was providing me with cover. When Stan fired back, I could tell he was on the starboard side. I moved up the port toward the bow. I knew we were only about five feet apart now.

Chapter 27

Diane reached Dave's house ten minutes later. She saw the front door was open. Then Dave walked out to the front porch with a beer and sat on a recliner.

Walter saw him and started wiggling. Then Dave's dog, Walter's son, came out of the house. Now Diane was fighting to hold Walter. He barked.

Dave turned their way. When he saw them, he stood and waved. He turned toward the open door and said something. Wanda appeared in the doorway. She grinned and waved enthusiastically.

Diane, who was being pulled by Walter, went to the porch. She let Walter go and he charged Waylon. Father and son were united again.

"Hey, Diane," Dave said. "Come on up here."

Diane stepped onto the porch and Wanda hugged her.

"Are you okay?" Wanda asked.

"Yeah, for now. I was wondering if I could leave Walter here for a while."

"Both of you can stay as long as you like," Dave said. "We've seen the news. They're lookin' for you and everyone now."

"Yeah, I know."

"We know you guys didn't do nothin' they're sayin.'"

"Thanks. I'm not going to stay," Diane said, "but I'd like to leave Walter for a few days."

"That's not a problem at all," Wanda said as she looked down at the two dogs who had discovered each other again. They were lying together on their sides and pawing at each other.

"Where will you go?" Dave asked before taking another pull from his beer bottle.

"I need to find Cam and make sure he's okay."

"On foot?" Wanda asked.

"For now. I'll try to get to my place and get my car."

"Bull hockey," Wanda said, waving her off. "They'll bust you as soon as you show up there. Take my car. We still have Dave's truck. I ain't using it."

Diane looked toward the driveway at the 2005 Firebird. It was wrecked slightly on the front left fender and the black paint was faded.

"I know it ain't much to look at, but it still runs like a bat outta hell."

"That'd be a great help, Wanda. Are you sure?"

"No problem. It uses regular."

She stepped back into the house and reappeared with the keys. Diane caught them when she tossed them to her.

"I'll take care of it," Diane said as she petted Walter who was still playing with Waylon.

She got in the car and turned the motor over. After a little grinding, it came alive with a roar. She backed out of the drive and honked as she pulled away.

I eased myself around the bow of the boat. Stan was still watching Jack. When I stuck the gun in his back, he froze.

"Drop the rifle and put both hands on the bow," I said as I moved back a step.

He didn't have any other choice. He dropped the gun and did as I said.

"Why were you two shooting at me?" he asked, turning his head to look at me.

"We know who you are and what you did," I said.

"I don't know what you're talking about. I was just out for a swim and you attacked me."

Jack pulled the boat to the beach beside Stan's boat. He came to us with his gun trained on Stan too.

"Are you guys here to rob me?" Stan asked.

"No, we're here to turn you over to the police," Jack said.

"For what?"

"For killing all those people on the beach."

"What beach?" Stan asked, smiling.

"Don't act dumb. You know what we're talking about," I said.

"I don't have a clue. How are you going to prove to the police that I did what you say I did?"

Jack and I looked at each other. We were wondering the same thing.

"I think the best thing for you to do is to let me go," Stan said, taking his hands off the bow and standing straight. He turned and looked at us. His facial features did resemble mine a bit. He was about my height and complexion. He could be mistaken for me when there was a gun pointed at you.

"Hello, Stan," Malinda said as she walked up behind us.

Stan's shoulders sank a bit. "Brittany," he said. "Did you come to save me from these thugs?"

"No, Stan. I'm here to kill you."

Stan looked totally submissive now. He knew she would do it. "How will you clear Cam's name if I'm dead?"

"We can compare your body to the film from the beach. It shouldn't be that hard."

"You know better than that. They already compared Cam's face to the film and are sure it was him. Without me alive to confess, you have nothing."

"And are you going to confess?"

"Not in a million years," he said and laughed.

"Where's Kailey?" I asked.

Malinda turned around to where she last saw Kailey. "She went after Holly. I heard two shots from that direction. I guess I had better go check on her."

When Kailey heard the gunshots ahead of her she ducked down in the scrub trees. *Someone else is here,* she thought. *Bexley.* Then she heard all the shooting from the beach and decided to turn back. Cam might be in trouble.

When she came out of the thicket, she saw Malinda, Jack, Stan, and Cam standing by the boats. She walked toward them.

She heard a shot from behind her and felt a tug on her leg. She dove back into the bushes.

Then she heard five more shots also from behind her. She could see the boat and the guys scattering. Stan fell to the ground; then she saw Jack grab his arm. Cam and Malinda had their guns out and were aiming back toward her and Bexley.

Kailey rolled onto her back and pulled her gun. She watched and waited for Bexley to show himself. Two bullets whizzed over her head. She heard someone moving quickly behind her. It was Bexley dodging the shots and finding a new hiding place. But he only gave away his position. Kailey aimed and fired. Bexley fell to the ground and didn't move.

She rolled back over and looked toward the beach. Cam and Malinda were standing next to the boat still aiming her way.

"Clear!" Kailey yelled.

They turned their attention to Jack.

"I'm okay," he said, but he was losing a lot of blood.

Malinda ripped her blouse and tied a tourniquet around Jack's upper arm. "We need to get him to a doctor," she said.

I looked down at Stan. He was staring blankly at the sky.

Kailey appeared next to us.

"What happened over there?" I asked.

"Bexley got Holly. I got Bexley. How's Jack?"

"He'll be okay if we get him to the hospital right away," I said.

"We'll take him," Malinda said. "You get in the boat and get out of here. You were never here. This was a war between Bexley, Holly, and Stan. The bullets in them came from Bexley's gun."

"Not the one in Bexley."

"I was working in a professional status. I was tracking him and got here when it was over."

I looked around the area at the carnage. "What about all the bullet holes in the back of his boat?"

"Who knows. Like I said, I got here when it was over and had to take out Bexley when he shot me in the leg."

That was the first time I noticed the blood running down her leg.

"How bad is it?"

"Just a scrape," she said, looking down at it for the first time.

"Malinda, you drive and get them both to the hospital," I said.

"Let's go," Malinda said. "Just leave the bodies here. I'll call the police."

I could hear sirens in the distance. "You won't have to," I said.

"Get in the boat and get out of here," Kailey said. "Take Jack's guns with you. We'll be okay."

I did as she said. When I pushed off and turned the boat, I saw a blue light flashing in the distance on the water. A sheriff's boat was coming our way.

I throttled forward full riding the waves out of the cove and turned port away from the police. I knew they could see me leaving. They would have to decide whether they wanted to chase me or get to the crime scene.

Chapter 28

Stacy called Stuart Bailey. He answered on the third ring. "Hello?" He didn't recognize the number.

"Hi Stu, it's Stacy."

"Stacy? Where are you?"

"I'm in Key West. Have you been looking for me?"

"I went to your boat today. Barbie wouldn't tell me anything. She said she hasn't seen you for a week."

"It's true, she hasn't. Why did you go looking for me?"

"I wanted to help you. Are you okay?"

"Yeah, I guess. I'm not hurt or anything, but I could use some help. Can I come to your house?"

He hesitated for a few seconds. "I had better come to pick you up. Do you have a place to hide until I get there?"

"Do you know Henry's Piece of Paradise on Atlantic Boulevard?"

"Yeah."

"I'm sitting at a picnic table under some trees in the parking lot."

"I'll be there in ten minutes. Don't move."

When they hung up, Stacy thought she had picked something up in his voice. She called Barbie to check out his story.

"Stacy, I've been trying to call you."

"My phone is gone. I've got this burner. What's up?"

"Stuart came by this morning looking for you. When he left, I watched him out the window. He met a police car at the top of the parking lot. I think he was going to turn you in."

Stacy's breath caught in her throat. She hurriedly looked around the area.

"Stacy?"

"I'm here," she said. "I just told him where I'm hiding. I gotta go."

She hung up and ran through the lot and across Atlantic Boulevard having to dodge several cars. She ran up George Street toward Garrison Bight, eleven blocks away.

Ahead of her, she could see blue lights coming her way. She turned into a residential yard and stood beside the house until they passed. Then she continued her run. That son of a bitch turned her in.

She wasn't sure where she was going or what to do when she got there. But she did know she needed a friend she could trust.

Sheriff Deputy Harding Neel was on his radio to the dispatcher.

"I see a boat leaving the area in a hurry. Request permission to pursue."

"We have units on the way to the beach, Harding; proceed with caution," the dispatcher said.

Harding turned his boat starboard and followed the boat from the beach.

I saw the sheriff's boat change direction. It was now after me. I kept the throttle wide open. There was a slight starboard quartering sea causing the boat to be airborne at times, but it handled the waves perfectly.

At the bottom of the horn, I turned to port and headed back up the Spanish Channel. The sheriff's boat was about a half-mile back, but he was closing the gap quickly.

I decided to ditch the guns before he caught me. I dropped them in the water one at a time. I would turn port to block his view each time I dropped one off the starboard side.

With that done, I looked for an escape route. When I passed Big Pine Key Park, I throttled back and turned into a canal. It was a residential area. Boats were sitting at their docks behind beautifully manicured lawns. It was a no-wake zone, but I pushed the throttle forward and skimmed over the smooth water.

I came to a connecting canal and turned port into it. A few blocks later it came to a dead end.

I had no choice now other than to abandon the boat and go on foot. I looked behind me and saw no sign of the sheriff's boat. I pulled to a dock and quickly tied the boat off. The house look empty so I walked through the yard and onto Hibiscus Drive in front of it. I was in a rural area now with very few homes. If the sheriff radioed in my location, I would be a sitting duck.

My cell rang. I checked it and saw it was Diane's new number. I answered it as I stepped into a wooded area and moved back where I wouldn't be visible from the road.

"Cam, where are you?" she asked.

I told her what had happened and that it didn't look good for me. "The sheriff is only a few minutes behind me. They'll more than likely check this area that they know better than I do and find me."

"I'm only twenty minutes from you. If you can hide that long, I'll pick you up."

I thought about it for a minute then said, "Then what? We can't hide forever. I don't want you involved in this."

"I already am involved. Just keep hidden. I'll be there soon."

We hung up and I watched the road from deep in the mangrove trees. I couldn't let Diane get caught with me in the car. She would face aid and abetting charges. That would only make matters worse.

A sheriff's car pulled onto the street and stopped at the end of the canal. He got out just as the sheriff's boat reached the end. The two men yelled something to each other and the one from the car turned to look around the area.

I called Diane back. "Don't come here. It's too late."

"No, it isn't, I'm almost there."

"Yes, it is," I said. I hung up the phone, dropped it on the swampy ground, and stepped out of the mangroves with my hands in the air.

The officer from the car saw me and drew his gun. He started walking toward me. I turned and knelt down on the pavement when he was about fifty feet from me.

Suddenly a car came around the corner and skidded to a stop between the sheriff's deputy and me. Malinda stepped out of the car with her CIA badge held up in plain sight.

She walked around the car and came to me. "CIA, you're under arrest," she said as she handcuffed me from behind.

"What's going on here?" the deputy yelled.

"This man is wanted by the CIA," Malinda said. "I'm taking him in. It's related to an ongoing investigation. Thanks for tracking him down."

Malinda put me in the back seat then climbed in, turned the car around, and drove away, leaving the two deputies staring.

A block later, I asked her what happened to Kailey and Jack.

"When the police arrived, an ambulance came with them. They're both being treated. I heard the police report on the radio and came after you. They relayed your position all the way here."

"What now?" I asked.

"Now I take you to the CIA holding cell for processing. There's nothing I can do about that, but I'll have you out in a day or two."

I leaned back in the seat and thought about how screwed up things had become in such a short time. I was out giving diving lessons to my beautiful friend Stacy and now my ex-wife was taking me to jail.

"Do I really have to go to jail?" I asked her.

"It would be the easiest way. But if for some reason you escaped, I could probably cover for you for a few days."

"What do you have in mind?"

"I don't know, maybe the car skidded off the road and I hit my head. If that did happen, my guess is Diane would pick you up only a block from here."

"So, you talked to Diane?"

"I talked to her from time to time," Malinda said.

"Malinda, don't do it," I warned her.

Suddenly the car went into a skid. It slid sideways, slowing just enough that no one would get hurt. It hit a tree broadside. Malinda was prepared for the collision as was I.

She tossed me the handcuff keys. "Get out now," she said.

Just then, a beat-up Firebird skidded to a stop next to us. I looked toward it and saw Diane behind the wheel. She waved for me.

"Malinda, you can't do this, you'll be in a lot of trouble."

"Cam, if you haven't noticed by now, I can do anything I want to do. My orders come from much higher than the director of the CIA. Just go, but stay out of sight."

"Malinda, you know how much I love you," I said sincerely.

"Go now, Cam."

I opened the door and stepped out into the freedom of the road. As I was about to close the door, Malinda said, "Cam, I love you too."

I got in the car with Diane and we sped away.

Chapter 29

"Mister Stiller," the deputy said, "what were you doing on the beach?"

Jack held his arm and winced in pain. Maybe a little more pain than he actually felt. After about fifteen seconds he said, "I came here in my boat. I was supposed to meet a girl. The next thing I knew, gunfire was erupting all around me. A stray bullet hit me in the arm. When the gunfire stopped, someone stole my boat and took off in it."

"Uh-huh," said the deputy. "Where is the girl you were supposed to meet?"

"That's what I'd like to know," Jack said. "Do you think she had anything to do with this?"

"I wouldn't have any idea about that. Is she the kind of girl who would be involved with murder?"

Kailey was listening to the conversation. When the ME finished bandaging her leg, she stepped over to them and said, "Don't ask him any more questions. He's in my charge and I'll question him."

She held up her CIA badge. "We've been tracking these drug dealers from Miami to Bermuda."

"So, the CIA is going to cover this case?" the deputy asked.

"Yes," Kailey said.

The deputy smiled. "Good deal, he's all yours and the dead guy and woman too."

"Two dead guys," Kailey corrected.

"Where's the other one?"

Kailey pointed at the bushes where she shot Bexley.

"We searched that area. There's no body there."

"There has to be," she said.

"No, there doesn't."

As the deputy walked away, he called over his shoulder to the other officers, "Wrap it up, boys. This is the CIA's case."

Stacy didn't stop running until she was standing in front of Jack's boat. She bent down and placed her hands on her knees and tried to catch her breath.

She stood and looked around the docks. There were a few fishermen at the end of the dock but no activities on any of the boats.

Stacy stepped onto Jack's boat and tried the door. It was locked. She sat down in his fishing chair on the rear deck.

"What am I going to do now?" she said softly to herself.

"Missy!" An older lady called to her from the dock.

Stacy stood and looked at her alarmed and wide-eyed.

"Are you a friend of Jack's?" she asked as she walked toward the boat.

"Yes, ma'am."

"Oh, I know you. You're that little friend of Cam's. I've seen you down here with him before. As a matter of fact, I've seen you on TV with him lately."

"I was just leaving," Stacy said and stepped off the fantail onto the dock.

"Now just wait a minute," she said. "I'm Bonnie, a good friend of Jack and Cam. You can't go wandering off from here. The police will catch you in no time. You come with me on down to my boat. You can stay there as long as you want. No one will find you there."

Stacy remembered Jack and Cam talking about Bonnie and had even met her once a few years ago. She knew she was a little quirky but a good person. Right now she didn't have much choice. Bonnie was her only chance.

"Thank you," was all she said.

"Come on then, let's go 'fore someone sees you."

"Will Malinda be okay?" Diane asked.

"She has connections. She'll get out of it. The problem is you're involved now. I didn't want that to happen."

"Everything that happens to you happens to me too."

"Take a right on 1, we're going to Marathon. I want to see if we can find a witness who was there when this went down. Now that Bexley, Stan, and Holly are all three dead, we don't have any way to clear ourselves."

I called John James in Marathon. "Can you contact the guy that took the movie with his phone?" I asked him.

"I don't think that would be a problem," John said. "What do you have in mind?"

"I'd like to meet with him. See if he recognizes me as the one who was actually there."

"I guess I can get him over here on other pretenses. I don't want to announce that you're going to be here."

"Thanks, John. We're about twenty minutes away."

"I'll open the gate. Who's with you?"

"Diane."

"When you come down Sombrero Drive, keep out of sight. The police are still thick around here."

"There's going to be more trouble too. I was just in a shoot-out in Big Pine. The ones who actually did the shooting on the beach were left dead on Long Beach."

"Do they know it was you?"

"Yes, I was chased in a boat. When they caught me, Malinda swooped in and took me into custody. Now here I am."

"You really know how to get into trouble, don't you?"

"I'm afraid so. This is one I don't know if I'll ever get out of."

"Let me make that call. I'll see you shortly," John said and hung up.

A couple of minutes later, my cell rang. It was Jack.

"Did you get away?"

"Not exactly, but Malinda got there before they could arrest me. I'm with Diane now on the way to Marathon."

"I hate to ask, but where is my boat?"

I gave him the location. "You might have to go to the police to get it. I don't know what they were going to do with it."

"We're still tied up at the beach. I'll check on it when we finish."

"Sorry about that."

"I've got more bad news," Jack said. "Bexley disappeared. I guess Kailey just wounded him."

"No sign of a trail?"

"We found a little blood. It led back to the parking area. I guess he left after the police came in."

"Great, I'll keep an eye out for him. Thanks for the update."

"No problem. I got a beep from your security camera a few minutes ago. Andy walked past your boat. I guess he was going fishing."

"I forgot you still have that on your phone."

"I ran it back to the morning you and Stacy left to go diving. It filmed the two of you getting ready to leave. It clearly shows that you weren't wearing the clothes they found in the bag."

"That could be our big break," I said excitedly.

"Well, it also shows you returning and leaving with the clothes in your hand."

"What? I didn't go back there and get any clothes."

"It sure looks like you did. The picture isn't high quality, but it looks like you."

"That must have been Stan. He came there and stole our clothes so he could later hide them in the boat."

"I don't know if this would hurt you or help you. It does look like you."

Then I thought about Andy and him saying he 'saw a man,' and that man looked like me.

"Can you talk to Andy? He told me several times he saw a man on my boat. When I asked what he looked like, he said, 'You.'"

"That might help. He'll probably be there fishing most of the day. He was carrying his lunch box. I'll get there as soon as I get my boat."

"Thanks, Jack, and sorry about the boat again."

"You owe me big time."

"I always do."

We crossed the Seven-Mile Bridge and turned right onto Sombrero Drive. When we approached the beach area, there were still a few police cars there, but the north end of the beach was open again.

I bent down and hid from view. The tinted windows of the old Firebird helped to hide me. Diane turned right and then left into the driveway. I heard the gate closing behind us.

The garage door opened and Diane pulled in. Once safely inside, I sat up. We'd be safe for a while.

John met us at the door. "Come on in, Carl will be here in a few minutes."

I filled John in on everything else that happened. I didn't want there to be any surprises. "So, we came here because we didn't know where else to go," I said.

"You did the right thing by coming here," John said.

"Is Rose home?" I asked.

"She's getting ready. Shes going to take Diane and go into town. I don't want either one of them to be here when Carl comes by."

"Good, I feel better without them here too," I said, looking at Diane.

"You don't have to worry about me, Cam," she said.

"I can't help but worry about you all the time."

Rose entered the room and hugged us. "Wanna go shopping, Diane?"

"Sure, I guess."

Rose led Diane back to the garage where they got into her Bentley GT Speed. I watched as they backed out of the drive and drove down the street toward the beach.

"Okay, John, what did you tell Carl?"

"I told him I wanted him to come by and talk about this movie. He doesn't know you're going to be here."

"I met him here at a party at your house a couple years ago," I said. "It has been a while, but I thought he would know it wasn't me at the beach."

John made us each a drink. We sat on the back veranda and watched the boats moving up and down the canal.

"Will Kailey's leg be okay?" John asked.

"I think so. She said it was only a flesh wound. I think Jack's arm will be sore for a while."

There was a knock at the front door. John excused himself and disappeared back inside the house.

When he returned to the veranda, he had Carl Law with him. When Carl saw me, his eyes widened.

"Don't be alarmed, Carl," John said. "He's here because I invited him."

"Don't you know the police are looking for him?" Carl said.

"They may be looking for him, but he's not the one you saw at the beach. That's why you're here. I want you to look him over closely. Is there anything about him that doesn't jive with the man you saw on the beach? Take your time and think about it. Then we'll look at the movie again."

Carl scratched his head. "Well, okay, I'll take a look."

I stood and Carl stared at me. He looked at my face and my hair.

"Not just his face, Carl," John said. "His whole body. The way he holds himself. The way he moves."

I walked around the veranda in my normal gait. I was hoping Carl would notice something different.

"Well, he even favors his right side like he did on the beach," Carl said.

"The man on the beach studied me. It would be easy for him to fake a slight limp," I said in my defense.

"I'm sorry, guys," Carl said. "The guy was waving a gun around and shooting. It makes it hard to focus on small details."

I pulled my gun from under my shirt and pointed it away from them. Carl jumped back.

"I'm not going to hurt you. I'm just giving you a feel for the situation again," I said.

He watched me move with the gun extended. Then he brightened.

"Is that the way you always hold your gun?" he asked.

"Yeah, normally," I said.

"I mean in your right hand."

"Yes."

"The guy on the beach, he held it in his left hand. I remember that."

"Let's look at the movie again," John said.

We huddled around the phone and played the movie. Carl was right. Stan was left-handed. Why had we not noticed that before?

"Carl, this guy's name is Stan Whittle," I said. "He was sent here to kill me or set me up for murdering these people. He was killed this morning by the other guy in the movie, John Bexley, who tried to kill me a few months ago. When my court day comes, will you testify that the guy was left-handed?"

"Sure, but do you think that would be enough to clear you? You know, your right side is a little tender. They might say you used your left hand because of that."

Now the jubilant feeling I had just had faded once more. He was right. I could have done that.

"Yeah, I guess that wouldn't be much of a defense."

"Do you have the body of the guy in the movie?" he asked.

"Yeah."

"Maybe that would be enough of a doubt."

"It might be."

"Do you have his gun? They could compare it to the one in the movie."

I thought back to Kailey handing me the guns to take with me in the boat when I left the beach. Did I take his too? If so, it was lying at the bottom of the Spanish Channel. The strong current could have washed it away to the Atlantic by now.

"I'm not sure."

"John," Carl said, "do you think Cam's innocent?"

"I know he is. No doubt in my mind."

"Then I believe it too. I'll keep studying the movie. I'll find something."

Chapter 30

Carl left the house promising to keep quiet about me being there. I believed he would.

By the time Diane and Rose returned, John and I had already come up with a plan to return to Key West.

"You're going to drive the car back to Key West. Return it to Dave and Wanda and get Walter. Take him to Jack's boat," I told Diane. "The three of you can take an extended cruise. Maybe go to the Bahamas."

"No way," she said. "I'm not going to leave you alone."

"Malinda and Kailey are here. I'll be in good hands."

"We'll talk about it on the way back to Key West," she said.

"I'm not going with you. John is going to take me by water."

Diane got a worried look on her face. She swept her long hair back with one hand and pulled a band from her pocket with the other, wrapping it around her ponytail. That was what she did when she was determined to get her way.

"You're going with me," she said.

"I don't want you to get stopped with me in the car," I said. "You'd be in too much trouble. I'm an escaped fugitive now. Even if they didn't think I murdered those people, I escaped from the CIA."

"But—"

"Please, this time, do as I ask," I pleaded.

"Where will you go?"

"John said I could stay in his condo there. I'll be safe."

"You know that sooner or later you're going to have to face the piper, don't you?"

"Yes, I know, but hopefully, by then, I'll have some proof that I'm innocent. I have to for Stacy's sake."

Her shoulders dropped in defeat. "Call me when you get there," she said.

"I will, now go."

Diane said her goodbyes and went to the garage. The car turned over for ten seconds before it finally came to life. A puff of blue smoke filled the garage.

She shrugged her shoulders and smiled then backed out into the street and drove away.

When she was gone, I told John I wanted to go to the beach and have a look at the crime scene.

"Are you crazy?" he said.

"The police are gone. We'll only be there for five minutes. I just want to get a feel for it."

"I'll go with you, but I'm going on record that I think this is a bad idea."

John gave me a ball cap to pull down over my eyes. We walked to the beach a block away. We were at the south end where it all took place. I didn't see any police even though some crime scene tape was still strung from the volleyball court to a tree near the fence.

"This is where Bexley and Mario Santana were sitting," John said, pointing at a picnic table.

"Mario Santana? Is he Alarico's brother?"

"I think so. Maybe cousin, I'm not sure."

"That's not going to go over very good," I said.

I scanned the area and got the feeling we were being watched. "Maybe you're right," I said. "This might not be a good idea."

We walked back to the house.

Valentine Galeas watched the two men who were standing on the beach. *I knew he would return.*

He made a phone call. "I have him. He's in a house one block from the beach. Send Recardo with the boat. Tell him I will call him if they leave by the water."

"Wanna beer?" Bonnie asked then burped. "'Scuse me."

"Have you got anything stronger?" Stacy asked.

Bonnie smiled. "I took you for a party girl. How about some of Cam's Wild Turkey?"

"Perfect," Stacy said.

While Bonnie was fixing the drink, Stacy thought about her next move. She had to do something to prove that she and Cam were innocent. Her hands were tied. If she went out in public she would probably be caught by the police. She wanted to call Ryan. He might tell her the latest on her status. Then she thought, *Better yet, I'll call Kailey.*

Bonnie handed her the drink. "Here ya go, sweetie."

"Thank you, I needed this."

"You're welcome. Cam and I have had a few drinks together sitting right here. Jack and I have had a lot of drinks together all over the marina."

"Do you go out to bars often?"

"I never go anywhere. I have my groceries delivered and Jack brings me booze when I get low. Which reminds me, he's been gone for a week. I need to catch him."

"I need to make a call. Is it okay if I step out onto the front deck?" Stacy asked.

"You go right ahead, a girl needs her privacy."

Stacy took her drink through the boat to the bow where she found a chair and sat. She called Kailey.

"Where are you?" Kailey asked.

"I'm with Bonnie. Do you know her?"

"Sure, she can be nice."

"I wanted to find out what has been happening and if I'm still running from the police, 'cause it sure seems like it."

"You don't want the police to find you if you can help it. You're supposed to be in my custody. As a matter of fact, I'll come there and pick you up in about an hour. I'm headed to Key West now."

"Thanks, that would be a big help."

Kailey filled her in on everything that had happened.

"So, the couple that really shot those people are dead?"

"Yes they are, but Bexley is still out there."

"I don't know how we're going to prove it wasn't us without them alive," Stacy said.

"We'll figure something out. See you in an hour."

John Bexley knocked on Dwayne Massy's door. When he answered it, he said, "John, I haven't seen you in a while. Come on in."

Bexley went into the room but had to lean on the door after he closed it.

"What's the problem? You don't look good."

Bexley pulled his lightweight jacket back. His shirt was covered with blood.

"Shot?" Dwayne asked.

Bexley nodded.

"Let's get you to the back room," Dwayne said and hooked an arm under his.

Dwayne Massy was known by the CIA as a man you could count on in just such an emergency. When John was in the CIA, he brought three different gunshot victims to him. They needed to be treated discreetly. Now he needed the same for himself.

"Lie down and let me take a look at ya," Dwayne said.

He cut Bexley's shirt and pulled it up to examine the wound. "The bullet went all the way through ya. I can tell by the wounds and the blood that you're one lucky son of a bitch. I don't think it hit any vital organs. You've lost some blood. You'll have to stay here a few days."

"I just got out of the hospital yesterday for this," he said and pointed to his shoulder, trying to sit up.

"Shit, I didn't even look up there. You must have someone who wants you dead."

"Yeah, more than one."

Dwayne laid John back down on the table and told him to lie still. He gave him an anesthetic and cleaned the wound.

"Yep, you were lucky," he said.

"I don't feel lucky."

"An inch to the right you wouldn't be lying here. You'd be lying in the street somewhere."

John's son Curt pulled into the drive as Carl pulled away. John had called him to take me to Key West.

We loaded a few things in his boat and idled away from the dock. Curt is an experienced sailor. I've been on some pretty high seas with him in the past.

I waved to John and gave him a thumbs up. I hoped he would be calling me with some good news after Carl had another look at the video.

The seas were calm and the sixty-foot Maritimo made it feel as if I were still on land.

A Coast Guard boat came up on our port side. I sat down in the salon out of sight. They hit their horn and waved at Curt. Luckily, they were just some friends saying hello.

We cruised past the Seven-Mile Bridge and moved farther away from the shore. The chops were a little heavier out there, but it was still a smooth ride.

"I have to say, Cam, I'm glad those two were killed, but it sure would help your case if they were in jail instead."

"Yeah, me too, Curt, and you're right. It would make things simpler. I suppose the CIA has the bodies by now. Surely they'll see the resemblance."

"From what I understand, they already know who they are. Didn't you say Kailey knew them?"

"She knew they were assassins, but we still can't prove they were at the beach."

"What you need to do is prove that you weren't."

Malinda waited until her car was on the wrecker before she left the scene with Agent Hunt.

"Brittany, I can't believe you just lost control on a country road like that," Hunt said.

"Shit happens. When I woke up, Cam was gone."

"I thought he was your friend."

"He is, but he has to prove his innocence. He knew I was taking him to jail and wouldn't be able to investigate."

"Well, he shouldn't be hard to find out here. Which way do you think he went?"

"How the fuck should I know? I was out. I'm going back to Key West. You find him."

"He's your prisoner."

"Not anymore. Drop me off at the rental agent. I'll get a car."

"Why is it you always pull some shit like this and never get in trouble?"

"I'm a lucky girl."

Chapter 31

Kailey pulled into Garrison Bight and stopped in front of Bonnie's boat.

"There's my ride, Bonnie. Thanks for everything," Stacy said and hugged her.

Bonnie walked to the car with her. She leaned down and told Kailey, "Hi. You take care of this little thing now."

"I will. Don't worry. Thanks for your help."

Stacy got in the car and Kailey drove away.

"I thought you were going to call your old boyfriend," Kailey said.

"I did. The fucker called the police on me. I almost got caught."

"You can't trust an ex."

"Shit, you can't even trust a current. I think they all think I'm guilty."

"I called Langley on the way here. They're satisfied that you're in my custody and they are sure Stan and Holly are the ones who shot up the beach."

"But?"

"But the local police aren't going to give up on you and Cam. Neither is the Marathon department. So we have to keep you hidden until Langley sends some more forceful agents down here to get you."

"To get me? Where will they take me?"

"A holding cell in a Federal prison."

"I can't do that. Cam needs me."

"Yeah, that's what I thought, so we aren't going to let them find you."

"Where are we going now?"

"Key West Bight."

"What's there?"

"My yacht. We're going to sail out of US waters. The crew is getting it ready now."

"What about the Coast Guard?"

"Arrangements have been made."

"It's getting dark. Will that be okay?"

"Yes, have you never been out on a ship at night?"

"The only boat I've been out on is Diane's skiff a few times with Cam."

"Girl, we have to get you out more often."

They arrived at Key West Bight and parked in the lot.

"Will you be okay here until I check out the boat?" Kailey asked. "I want to make sure no one is watching it."

"Sure. Call me when you want me to come."

Kailey walked to the main dock and turned toward the boat.

"Kailey," Ryan said from behind her.

She stopped and waited for him.

"What do you want?" She sounded disgusted.

"Do you know where Stacy is?"

"I swear, Ryan, if you don't lay off that girl..."

"What will you do, sick your CIA friends on me?"

"If I wanted to take you down, I wouldn't need any friends," she growled.

He backed off a bit. There was something in her eyes that scared him a little.

"Look, I'm sorry," he said. "I just want to be the one who finds her so I can make sure she doesn't get hurt."

"She's in the custody of the CIA. You and the rest of the department don't have any authority to capture her. If you do, it will be the same as breaking her out of jail. She's already under arrest. She's being held in a secure environment and won't be hurt."

"Kailey, you know this isn't over. She'll be here in court and the longer she's on the run the more dangerous it is for her."

"She's not on the run. She's a Federal prisoner. Can't you get that into your head?"

Ryan stared at Kailey for a minute then turned and walked away. She watched him until he was out of sight. She saw his headlights come on in the lot as he drove away.

She went to the boat. It was ready to go so she called Stacy and told her to come quickly.

Curt was piloting the boat while I went over the movie again. I had to find something out of place.

"We have a boat coming up quick on the starboard side," Curt said.

I looked over the gunwale and saw a twenty-six-foot Century center console boat coming at us. The man standing in front had his eyes on us.

"Do you have any guns on board?" I asked Curt.

"Storage closet on your right. Bring me one too."

I opened the closet. It looked like a gun safe inside. I chose two automatic M-16s. I didn't know where they came from, but I was sure they weren't legal.

"Here ya go," I said, handing him one.

"Good choice. I hope we don't need them."

That's when the glass broke out in the window next to Curt's head.

"Get down!" I yelled.

Curt shut the throttle down and left the pilothouse. We kneeled behind the gunwale and waited. Bullets kept ricocheting off the boat.

When we knew they were close, we both rose up at the count of three and opened fire on them. They were only twenty yards away. The man in the front fell immediately.

The other tried to turn his boat away but was going too fast. He panicked and ran into the side of our boat.

The impact threw him to the deck unconscious.

I checked the damage to Curt's boat first. It was cracked but above the water line. The Century was sinking.

I jumped down into it and grabbed the driver, handing him to Curt. As I was stepping back to our boat I felt my foot getting wet. By the time I was on board, the boat was gone along with the man we shot.

"Who the hell are these guys?" I asked.

Curt knelt down next to the unconscious man and checked his pockets for ID. There was none.

"My guess is you were spotted at the beach. This has to be one of Santana's men."

"Shit, now I have the cartel after me too."

Diane arrived back at Dave's house. It was dark, but the two of them were sitting on the porch drinking beer with the porch light on when she pulled into the driveway. They waved.

"Hey, Diane!" Dave yelled.

So much for a good place to hide.

Walter looked up and started to bark when he saw her.

She got out of the car and went inside, turned the light off, and came back out.

"No one's supposed to know I'm here," she said.

"We didn't know you was coming home," Wanda said.

"Yeah, I guess not."

Walter was wiggling his whole body. She leaned down and petted him. " Hey, big guy, did you miss me?"

"Him and Waylon had a good time today. I took 'em everywhere," Dave said. "Everyone wanted to know where Cam was though. I said I haven't seen him."

"You took Walter out in town?"

"Yep."

Diane looked up and down the street. If anyone who was looking for Cam saw Walter, they'd know Cam was around. To prove that fact, it didn't take long before the street was full of police cars.

There was no sense in running. Diane just sat on the porch and watched the display of four police cars emptying out officers with their guns pointed at the house.

"What the fuck?" Wanda said. "Did they follow you here?"

"No, they followed Walter here."

"My bad," Dave said.

Then the megaphone came to life. "Everyone on your knees with your hands laced behind your heads!"

The three of them did as they were told.

Two officers came to the porch. "Where's Cam Derringer?" one asked.

"I haven't seen him in a couple of days, since you idiots started chasing him," Diane said.

He turned and called to the others, "Search the house!"

Four officers with their guns drawn stepped around the threesome and burst through the front door.

"He's not here," Diane said. "And you're after the wrong guy."

"Diane, I hate to tell you, but Cam was pulled over in Marathon the same day of the shooting. Why was he there if he was supposed to be diving down here?"

Cam didn't say anything about being pulled over. This was new and disturbing. She knew he went there, but she didn't know they knew.

"He went there after they finished diving. He went to investigate. But when he got there, he heard he was a suspect, so he left."

"Why would he go there to investigate?"

"You'll have to ask him. Now can we get up? You don't have anything on us."

The others came back out of the house. "No sign of 'im inside."

"He hasn't been here," Dave said.

"Why is Walter here?" the officer asked.

"They were watching him for me," Diane said.

"Where have you been?"

Now what? She thought a bit. "The CIA has been questioning me."

"We can check on that."

"Kailey Arlington," Diane said.

He waved all the men back to their cars. "We're watching you, Diane. I know Cam will be back soon and we'll get 'im."

He turned and left. They were still on their knees when the patrol cars rolled down the street.

They got up finally and sat back down in the chairs before they spoke.

"That was cool," Dave said.

"Yeah, we got a story to tell," Wanda chimed in.

Diane pulled out her phone and called Kailey.

Chapter 32

"He's coming around," I said.

The man lying on the deck was starting to move. We were still headed for Key West. It was going to be hard for Curt to explain why he was on the boat and how the boat was damaged.

He opened his eyes. They widened when he realized who was standing over him. He pointed at me and said, "I saw you. You killed Mario Santana. You will die. His brother will not stop before you are dead."

I didn't see any point in arguing that it wasn't me with this guy.

"Can you swim?" I asked him.

"He jerked around and looked out toward the swim platform. "We are miles from the shore," he said.

"Then I suggest you lie there and keep your mouth shut."

He did exactly that.

I called Malinda on the way. She said she was in Key West but would meet us at the Stock Island Yacht Club to collect the prisoner.

It was dark when we docked at the club. Malinda was waiting for us. She tossed a pair of handcuffs to us and told me to put them on him.

"What good do you think this is going to do? Santana will see you dead before morning," he said.

"No, he won't," Malinda said. "I talked to him a while ago. He said he would give you two days to prove you're innocent, Cam. After that, it'll be war."

"Well, that's something," I said. "Thanks."

"What do you mean prove your innocence? I saw you."

"It wasn't me," I said. "He's all yours, Brittany."

The man's eyes widened again. "Brittany? You are *that* Brittany?"

"Yes, she is," I said.

The man shut up and went along peacefully.

"I'll see you in a while, Cam," Malinda said as they were leaving.

We pulled out of the marina and cruised around to Key West Bight. The first thing I noticed was Kailey's yacht was gone. It left a large hole in the marina.

I called her and told her we were docking in the marina.

"I have Stacy with me. We're outside US waters. Ryan was waiting for me when I got there. Be careful."

"I'll keep you updated. I haven't heard anything from Bexley. You must have hit him pretty good."

"Yeah, I thought he was dead. I must be slipping in my old age."

"Yeah, you are thirty-four now."

"I love you," she said.

"I love you too. We'll be back together before too long."

We waited another hour before leaving the boat. When we did, the bars were jumping. There was a cruise ship in town. It was a good cover for me. I just wished I wasn't six foot four.

We went to the Hyatt Key West Resort where Curt and John owned a condo. It was spacious and overlooked the bay.

"I'm not going to stay," Curt said. "Will you be okay?"

"Yes, thank you very much. Tell your father to send me the bill for the boat."

"It's insured. Hit and run the way I see it."

"I insist."

"I'll tell him."

"I'm going to call Jack to come to stay here. Is that okay?"

"Not a problem. Just stay out of sight."

Curt left the room and I called Jack. "How's the arm?"

"Not bad considering all I had to go through today."

"What do you mean?"

"The police had the boat. I had to go to the station and fill out a thousand pages of paperwork before they would give it back to me. Then I was interrogated about why I was there in the first place."

"Crap, Jack, you did have a bad day."

"No thanks to you, *again*."

He sounded a little mad.

"Well, I'm at the Hyatt in Curt's condo. I was just wondering if you would like to join me."

I held the phone away from my ear a bit waiting for the screaming to start.

"I'll be there in a half-hour," he said and hung up.

I could always count on Jack. He could always count on me—to get him in trouble. I vowed to myself to try to do better.

"Hi, Diane," Kailey said. "Where are you?"

"I'm at Dave's, but the police were just here."

"They didn't arrest you. That's a good thing. I guess you're free to move about now."

"I guess. Cam's here now too."

"Yeah, I just talked to him. He's at the Hyatt."

"Curt's condo?"

"Yes, but I would call before I went there and then make sure you're not being followed."

"How's Stacy?"

"She's faring well. She wants this to be over with like the rest of us do. I hate to be out here away from all of you, but I felt it was the best for her."

"You're absolutely right. We can handle things here and Malinda's here too."

"Keep me informed," Kailey said.

"I will."

Diane did feel better now knowing the police weren't after her. They knew she was in the Hamptons when all this occurred. It was just a boat like hers that was used in the crime.

"Thanks for the loan of the car," she told Wanda. "It was a big help."

"No problem, girl. Wanna ride home?"

"I better call a cab. You might have had too many beers."

"Only five or six. Hell, the evening's young."

"I don't want to put you out all the same," Diane said and hit the button on her phone for the cab.

While she waited for the cab, she called Cam.

"Hello Diane," I answered, recognizing her new phone again.

"Can I come over?" she asked.

"Are you clean?"

"I don't think I'm being followed."

"Is Walter with you?"

"Yes."

"Aren't you afraid someone will spot him?"

"I hadn't thought about that. It would be the same thing Dave did. A lot of people on the island know Walter and me. I'll take Walter to my house then I'll be there," she said.

"Call Jack. He's getting ready to come here. You might be able to catch him in time to come with him."

"Okay, bye," she said and hung up.

I called the restaurant at the resort and had a cheeseburger and fries delivered to the room. I finished it before Diane and Jack arrived.

"I see you caught him in time," I said.

"Barely. He was almost here, but he came back and got me. We brought you a steak sandwich. Thought you'd be hungry."

"I'm starving. Thank you," I said and started in on it.

Even though I had just eaten this was one hell of a sandwich and needed to be eaten too.

Jack checked the fridge and found a beer for Diane and a cold bottle of vodka for us.

"How do you want it?" Jack asked.

"On the rocks," I said.

He handed me the drink and sat down on the sofa with Diane.

"What's our next move?" Diane asked.

"That I don't know," I answered her, trying to smile. "I guess we need to find Bexley before he finds us."

"I don't have anything to hide now," Diane said. "I can check the veterinarian offices and hospitals. He was going to need treatment somewhere."

"That's a good idea, but don't confront him if you find him."

"I won't and I'm going to do it tonight. He may be released by tomorrow."

"Jack, you can go with her," I said.

"I'll be okay. I want you two to stay together. You always find trouble," she said to me. "It would be a good idea to have Jack for backup."

"Then I'd get in trouble again," Jack said.

"That's not necessary," I said. "Malinda will be here in a few."

I finished my sandwich and my drink and then stood. "When Malinda gets here, I'm going to go out myself and search for him. I know a few spots where he might go that aren't exactly in the Yellow Pages."

"Wait, it sounds like you're looking for trouble," she said.

"I guess I am. Before trouble finds me."

"Keep in contact with me," she said.

"You too."

When Diane and Jack left, I stepped out onto the veranda and sat in a chair. The night was a little breezy and the humidity was low, for here anyway. It felt good. I wished all this was over. It had disrupted everyone's life.

"A penny for your thoughts," Malinda said from behind me.

I had left the door unlocked. Not a good move.

"Have a seat," I offered.

She did, next to me. "I ran into Diane and Jack in the parking lot. Just where is it you're planning to find Bexley?"

"The old haunts. The Beck Building, Ramon's, and Dwayne Massy's."

"Those do sound like good starting places. I'd probably go to one of them if I needed help," she said.

"I'm ready if you are," I said.

"Do we have to be in such a hurry? We have the place to ourselves."

I thought about it a bit and said, "Normally, I wouldn't pass up the opportunity to have sex with you. But I can't focus on anything else right now. I'm afraid I wouldn't be there for ya."

"Has Kailey finally gotten to you?"

"She has, but she told me that anytime I wanted to be with you, she would understand. No one else, just you."

"I'd do the same for her. I love that girl."

"Yeah, me too."

"Let's go then."

We used Malinda's car and headed for the Beck Building first. Doctor Marrett has an office on the second floor. He's discreet about his after-hour patients and charges them heavily for the service.

"The building's dark," I said.

Malinda bent down to look up at his window. The shades were drawn, but we could tell there was no light behind them.

"Instead of checking this one out, let's go to the others to see if there's any sign of life," she said.

"Okay. If we don't see any, we'll start knocking on doors."

We drove to Dwayne's house. The lights were on so we parked a block down and walked back keeping to the shadows.

Malinda walked down the side of the house while I watched the front door. I saw her on her tiptoes looking into a window. She came back to me and whispered, "There's a bed in that room. It's covered with blood. He just had someone in there."

"You take the back door; I'll take the front. You knock; I'll bust the door in."

"Why don't we try to be a little quieter about it?" she said. "I'll try to pick the lock on the back door and we'll both walk in."

That did sound a little safer, so I agreed. We walked to the back of the house. I stopped and looked into the window on the way by. I didn't have to stand on my tiptoes to see through the blinds.

Malinda pulled a little kit from her pocket and started to work on the lock. I heard it click five seconds later.

"Ready?" she asked.

I nodded. She eased the door open and I walked in first with my gun pointed in front of me.

Dwayne was sitting at the kitchen table, drinking a cup of coffee.

"He already left," he said. Then he saw Brittany walk in behind me. "Hi, Brit."

"Dwayne, mind if we take a look?" she asked.

He waved his arm toward the rest of the house welcoming us to check it out.

We toured the house. It was empty. We returned to the kitchen.

"I told him not to leave so soon. He's not in the best of conditions," Dwayne said. "I've seen the news. I thought you'd be here. I tried to keep him here until you arrived. I never did like that son of a bitch."

"Any idea where he went?"

"Sorry, none."

"Put your hands in the air, Cam," a voice said from the doorway.

I turned to see a tall, bulky policeman standing at the door. Behind him, I could barely see two more around his large form.

I looked back at Dwayne. "I didn't call 'em," he said.

"John Bexley called us," the officer said. "He said that man who tried to kill him would be here."

"This man is in my custody," Malinda said, showing her CIA badge.

"Not this time, Brittany. We have a warrant for his arrest. You'll have to take it up with the judge."

Another officer, Jimmy Ward, who I know and play poker with on occasion, stepped into the room. "Sorry, Cam," he said. "I have no choice." He patted me down and removed the gun from my belt. Then he loosely slipped handcuffs on me. "Let's go."

"I'll be down there when you arrive," Malinda said. "I'll make some calls on the way."

I was booked, fingerprinted, and locked in a holding cell at the station. I knew Malinda wouldn't be able to come to the station in person for the threat of being recognized as my ex-wife. She'd already taken too many chances.

I was right. Agent Geraldo Toribio showed up an hour later insisting that I be released into his custody. The sergeant on duty told him, "No way."

It looked as though I was going to be the guest of the Key West Police Department for a while.

"He'll have an arraignment in the morning. Then we'll see if you can have him," the sergeant said.

"Will Bexley be there?"

"I don't know. He should be."

Geraldo said a few curse words under his breath, told me not to worry and left.

Me? Worry?

Chapter 33

Malinda called Kailey and gave her the bad news. "Plus, Bexley is still out there," she said.

"Do you want me to come back there?"

"No, I think you should keep Stacy safe for as long as we can. At the arraignment tomorrow we're going to show the judge the pictures of Stan and Holly. If we can get him to understand the whole situation, maybe he'll at least let him go into our custody."

"I hope so. I don't know if we can prove he wasn't there."

"Another thing," Malinda said "He was pulled over the same day in Marathon by a sheriff's deputy."

"Oh, crap. He was there to see Curt."

"Yeah, and he said he would never tell the reason for his visit to Marathon. He doesn't want to get Curt or John involved. This isn't good. They have him at the scene," Malinda said. "Just keep Stacy occupied and maybe it would be a good idea not to tell her about this yet."

"Yeah, you're probably right. No need to add more worry for her. I'll take her diving tomorrow."

"Good, I'll keep you informed."

Malinda returned to her hotel and slipped on the black wig she sometimes wore. She needed to find Bexley. He was the only one left who could tell the police that Stan was disguised as Cam. More than likely, though, he never would. In that case, he needed to die anyway.

If Bexley showed up for the arraignment the next day, she'd follow him afterward. But she had her doubts about that. Tonight, she'd just check the streets and call the hotels. There wasn't much of a chance she'd find him, but she had to do something.

She walked to the parking lot but then decided to walk into town instead of driving. With the crowd, she wouldn't find a spot to park anyway, and she was in the heart of town now.

It felt good to be walking down the street she had spent so many days and nights on with Cam. She missed those days and sometimes dreamt of how nice it would be if they were back now. Cam was always in some kind of danger and she knew a lot of the cause was from her and Kailey. One incident led to another. Maybe he would be better off if they both left and never returned.

She pushed those thoughts out of her head and went to the first hotel on her list. After checking with the desk, she realized she was wasting her time. Bexley could be anywhere. This town had hundreds of hotels and inns.

John Bexley watched Brittany checking the hotel. How did she know to come to this one?

He decided to follow her. She had been a pain in his side for too long. It was time to put a stop to her regime.

Malinda headed back to her hotel. As she was walking through the parking lot, she heard a pop and felt a thud in her back. She'd been shot from behind. The last thing she remembered was thinking how stupid she was to let her guard down.

A deputy came to my cell and walked me to the courtroom at ten a.m. Judge Norman Mantel was presiding that morning. He was a fair man whom I had been in front of a few times as a defense lawyer.

My attorney was Stuart Johnson, a man I have trusted for many years. He warned me that they had a good case against me but he would see to it that I got the best representation I could get.

"We're not going to let them railroad you," he said.

I looked around the courtroom for Malinda and hoped she wouldn't be there. She wasn't. Neither was Agent Toribio. It looked like it was me, Stuart, Diane, and Jack.

"Mister Derringer," the judge said, "this is not a trial, as you're very aware. We're here today to see if we have sufficient evidence to hold you for a trial. You know the workings of the court so we'll skip some of the formalities. Does the prosecution have an opening statement?"

"Yes, Your Honor. This man, Cam Derringer, was seen at Sombrero Beach on the day of the shootings. The witness, John Bexley, positively identified him as the shooter along with his girlfriend Stacy Monroe who is still at large. Other witnesses say they heard Bexley call him Cam and that Cam himself called for Stacy to turn the boat around."

"Is John Bexley in the courtroom today?" the judge asked.

"No, Your Honor."

The judge looked at us now. "Stuart, your turn."

"Your Honor, Cam and Stacy were out in the middle of the Atlantic scuba diving at the time of the shooting. Attempts on his life have been made since then. Two people were shot by John Bexley who were the actual shooters. The CIA was on the scene at the time of the shooting and can show the intent. The two who were killed matched the description of Cam and Stacy. It would have been easy for them to make people believe they were looking at them on the beach when everyone was running and frightened. The couple are assassins known to the CIA."

"Is a representative of the CIA in the courtroom today?" the judge asked.

Stuart looked around the room. "No, Your Honor."

The judge shook his head. "Neither one of you has much. Why didn't you get your witnesses together before you came in here today?"

"We did," Stuart said. "I don't know what happened."

"Same here, Your Honor. Bexley was supposed to be here."

"Do you think that maybe the fact that he killed two people is why he isn't showing up?" the judge said angrily.

The courtroom door opened and Agent Geraldo Toribio walked in. "Sorry I'm late, Your Honor," he said then came to our bench.

"Cam, I hate to tell you this but Brittany was shot in the back in her hotel parking lot last night. She's in serious condition at KWMC."

"No," I said. "Will she make it?"

"Right now, it doesn't look good. She's in recovery but weak."

Agent Geraldo Toribio turned to the judge. "Your Honor, the agent in charge was shot in the back last night. We're searching for John Bexley who we think did it. He was last seen in the area last night by Doctor Dwayne Massy. He had an operation to perform this morning and couldn't make it to court. I have a statement from him. May I?" he asked, holding the paper up to the judge.

The judge waved him forward with his fingers. "Can no one show up for court nowadays?"

The judge read the paper and handed it back to Geraldo. "It doesn't prove anything, but it shows him in the area with a gunshot wound."

"Your Honor," Stuart said, "all the evidence shows there is doubt as to Cam's guilt. The prosecution only has a witness who is wanted for murder and a few people who said they heard someone call the names Cam and Stacy."

"Your Honor, we have one more piece of evidence today," the prosecutor said. "We found the clothes they were wearing at the beach in Cam's daughter's boat, which was the boat used in the attack."

The judge let out a heavy sigh and deliberated a few minutes looking over the evidence. "I don't think we have sufficient evidence to charge Cam Derringer with the murders of six people at the beach. But I'm going to hold him in custody for twenty-four hours while the two of you get your acts together. If nothing new is presented at that time, he will be set free."

I leaned over to Stuart and whispered in his ear.

He stood again. "Your Honor, Mister Derringer has asked permission to visit the agent in the hospital whom Bexley shot in the back last night."

The judge shook his head slightly. "Is she a relative?"

Stuart looked at me. I wanted to say, "Yes, she's my wife," but I knew I couldn't put her identity in jeopardy. "She's a very dear friend, Your Honor," Stuart said.

"I'm sorry she was shot, but I can't allow that at this time. We'll keep you updated on her condition. Anything else?" the judge said.

No one had anything so he adjourned the court. No one won that day, but I felt as if I had lost big time.

Chapter 34

Kailey and Stacy dropped down into the waters near Water Cays in the Bahamas. It's a beautiful coral reef and was easy access from the yacht.

Stacy felt like a pro now as she dropped through the water. Kailey didn't have to guide her or signal for her to do anything. She was a free spirit for now, but she kept thinking about Cam and the last time she dove.

Kailey was taking pictures. She turned the camera on Stacy. She posed in various comical moves. Kailey gave her a thumbs up.

A half-hour later they were climbing onto the swim platform.

"That was beautiful," Stacy said.

"Yes, and those pictures of you are going to be priceless."

They laughed and climbed onto the fantail. "We'll check them out on the laptop in a few minutes," Kailey said. "How about a glass of champagne first?"

"Wow, is that the way the rich and famous live?"

"Sometimes."

Kailey walked to the bar and flipped the laptop up on the way. She hit a key and went on to fix the drinks.

Stacy was watching the laptop come to life. When it did, she appeared on it doing all her funny moves.

"How in the hell did you get that on there so quickly?" she asked.

"I have a satellite camera. It records straight to my laptop."

"Mine's satellite too," Stacy said, "but I'd never know how to set that up."

"You don't have to. If it was on your Wi-Fi when you first turned it on and put in your info it'll feed to your laptop."

"I didn't know that," she said.

They watched the whole dive again. It wasn't as beautiful on the camera as it was being there, but it was pretty amazing.

"Another?" Kailey asked, picking up the empty champagne glass.

"Why not, it might be my last dive as a free woman."

"Not a chance. We'll make sure you don't go to prison."

"I don't know. I wonder how Cam's doing. If he's having any luck finding Bexley."

Kailey sat next to Stacy and placed her hand on Stacy's knee. "I wasn't going to tell you this yet, but Cam was arrested yesterday. He had an arraignment this morning. They didn't have enough evidence to file charges, but the judge is giving them until tomorrow to come up with proof."

"We should be there to help him," Stacy said.

"If we were there, we would only add to his problems. He'd worry about us. He told me to keep you gone as long as it takes to prove you weren't there."

"I'm sitting out here on a yacht drinking champagne and Cam's in jail. That's just not right and you know it."

"Do you think it would help if you were in jail too? Because you would be."

Stacy sat back in her chair and downed her glass of champagne. "Can't you think of something we can do?"

Kailey realized she was right. They needed to get back to Key West. Cam needed their help more than ever before.

"I'll tell the captain to get underway," Kailey said. "We'll be in Key West this afternoon."

Her phone rang. "Yes?" she answered.

"Kailey, it's Diane. Malinda was shot in the back last night."

The nurse went out into the hallway and called for the doctor. "She's awake!"

The doctor came into the room and checked the monitors. "Everything looks good. She might just come out of this after all."

"Her blood pressure is rising to normal," the nurse said.

"Brittany, can you hear me?" the doctor asked.

She looked toward the doctor and gave a weak smile.

"Can you follow my finger with your eyes?" he asked and moved his finger back and forth in front of her.

"Very good. Now, you get some rest and I'll be back to check on you shortly."

As the doctor was leaving the room he heard her mumble something softly under her breath. He stopped and returned to her bedside.

"What is it, Brittany?"

"Bexley," she said faintly and fell back asleep.

I asked the jailer if I could have my laptop since I wasn't charged with any crimes. He came back a few minutes later and said the judge had agreed to let me have it.

Jack went to the boat and picked it up and returned a few minutes later.

"What do you think you're going to find?" he asked.

"I figure John Bexley is hurting badly. He can't keep running around Key West. No one can rest here. I want to find out where he's from and if he has any family close by."

"I could have done that for you," he said.

"I want you to keep checking the area. Malinda must have been close to him last night. If he's around here, he shouldn't be hard to spot. Maybe she was checking the local hotels."

I brought up a picture of him from the CIA site on the internet. They hadn't changed it since he left.

"Take the laptop out to the office and sweet talk one of the young girls into printing this pic out," I said.

"I don't have to sweet talk anyone, Cam. Someone will do it for me."

Jack left and returned a couple minutes later. "Here ya go," he said. "I had four made in case we need them."

Once back on my laptop, I started to google his name and career. His hometown wasn't on the CIA site for obvious reasons. I had to go all the way back to his college days when he played football for South Carolina.

"John Bexley, TE, runs ninety-five yards for the winning touchdown against Alabama."

It went on to say he was being looked at by scouts and his hometown of Orlando, Florida was proud to claim him as one of their own. The high school he attended was cheering him on.

"He's from Orlando," I told Jack. "That doesn't mean he went home, but he might."

I read a little further to find out he blew out a knee. He didn't make it big time in football. After his knee healed and he graduated, he joined the South Carolina Police Department.

"I wonder what made him change from being an agent to running the cartel in Bermuda with Camata," Jack said.

"The money. It changes a lot of people. He saw how much Camata was making and how they couldn't touch him. It was too tempting."

Jack left to show his picture around the local hotels and bars. He started with the Hyatt where Malinda was to be staying last night.

"No, he doesn't look familiar," the woman at the desk said. "But I wasn't working here last night when the shooting happened."

She turned around in her chair and called to someone in another room. "Debbie, who was working last night?"

"Samone!" came the answer from the ghost voice.

She turned back to me. "Samone," she said. "She'll be in tonight."

Jack thanked her and moved on to the next hotel. The third hotel he came to, Ocean Breeze Resort, gave him hope.

"Yes, sir. He's staying here," the woman said after Jack told her what it was about. "Did he have something to do with the shooting?"

"That's what we're trying to find out," Jack said. "Can you tell me which room he's staying in?"

"I'm not supposed to give that information out. I already told you too much."

"There is a reward for his capture," Jack lied.

Her eyes brightened. "How much?"

"Five thousand for information leading to his arrest."

He knew it should have been higher, but if he actually caught Bexley here at the hotel, he'd want to come up with the cash for her.

She looked behind her and then down at the computer screen.

"Two zero six," she said.

"Thank you," Jack said and waited for her to point the way.

She pointed to her left and whispered, "The elevator is down that hall. Take a left on the second floor."

Jack walked to the elevator and found the steps next to it. He climbed the stairs to the second floor and turned left. Two zero six was three doors down. It was also ajar.

Jack drew his gun and moved to the door. He peeked through the opening. Suddenly the door flew open and a small Mexican woman screamed when she saw Jack standing halfway in the room.

"Sorry, sorry," Jack said, holding his empty hand up and hiding his gun behind his back.

She put her hand to her breast. "You scare me," she said.

Jack looked into the room. The sheets were off the bed and the pillowcases lay on the floor with them.

"Where's the man who stays here?" he asked.

"Gone. Blood on sheets. Bad man. He leave last night."

Jack entered the room. He checked the waste basket and the drawers. There were no clues as to who stayed there or where they might have gone.

He apologized to the woman again and left the room.

Bexley was going to have to find someplace to hide. He was still bleeding from Kailey's shot. Maybe Cam was on to something. Maybe it was time for Bexley to go home.

Jack started to make mental plans to go to Orlando. He knew it would be easier if Cam was able to go with him, but unless he was released tomorrow, Jack would be going alone.

Chapter 35

That evening, when Deputy Rollins brought my supper, I asked him if there were any new developments.

"I haven't heard anything, Cam. I do know there has been nothing come across the desk for the judge to look at. I'll keep an eye out for you though. It's just not right to be holding you with no evidence."

"Yeah, I agree, and there can't be any evidence because I wasn't there."

"Sixteen more hours and you'll be out. We're searching for Bexley ourselves. The whole department is behind you. God knows you've helped us out a few times."

"Thanks, Rick."

Five minutes after he left, Jack showed up. He told me about the hotel and Bexley leaving the night before.

"Wait until tomorrow. If I get out we'll take my plane and go," I said.

"Okay. Good luck with it."

While we were talking, Deputy Rollins came back in. "Cam, they say there's a movie of the massacre at the beach. The prosecution says you're on it plain as day."

"Yeah, I've seen it. It was a good setup, but it's not me."

"I just wanted to let you know."

"Thanks," I said, but I felt deflated. I'd been hoping it wouldn't show up.

"It's okay, Cam. We can point out the similarities between Stan and Holly and you and Stacy. It might even work in our favor."

"Yeah, maybe," I said, but I didn't feel it. "Why don't you go check on Diane? With Bexley out there, I'm not comfortable leaving her alone."

"Okay, Cam, but don't worry. We'll fix this."

He left and an hour later Stuart came to the cell.

"I guess you saw the film," I said.

"Yes. Did you know it was out there?"

"Yes, if it's the same one. I saw it on the first day."

"You should have told me about it. I could have been prepared."

"Do you have it with you?"

"Yes, it's on this thumb drive," he said, pulling it out of his pocket.

I slid it into my laptop. It was different from the one Curt had shown me but the context was the same right down to the name on the back of the boat.

"This is damning, Cam."

"Does it help to know that I'm right-handed and this guy is left-handed like Stan?"

"Well, that is some doubt, but we're going to need more."

Kailey and Stacy landed in Key West Bight. Stacy didn't leave the boat. It was still too dangerous to be seen. Kailey went to see Cam.

"I agree with Jack," she said. "This might work out to our advantage."

"I just don't see how."

"He's a good double but not a perfect one. We'll find something. Let's look at it again."

We did, several times. It was obvious to us that it wasn't Stacy or me at the beach, but it might not be for a jury.

"Stuart's working on it. Where's Stacy?"

"She's on the boat. I told her not to leave and showed her a good hiding place."

"Good, but I would feel better if the two of you were still out at sea."

"I had to come back for Malinda. I'm heading to the hospital now. I'll give you a call when I know something."

"Thanks, give her my love."

"I will."

Stacy sat on the boat going over everything in her head. If only someone would have seen them out diving. She kept thinking about the boat that was anchored a few hundred yards away, the crew of which kept the other boats away. *That boat had to be a part of the operation to frame us,* she thought.

Then another thought hit her. She needed to call Barbie.

"Are you ready, Cam?" the deputy asked me at ten a.m.

"I guess. As ready as I'll ever be."

We entered the courtroom and sat at our table. I looked over at the prosecutor who had a big grin on his face. *I'd like to wipe that off,* I thought.

The judge came in. He wasn't smiling. I didn't like that either.

After the formalities, he asked, "Is there any new evidence?"

The prosecutor sprang to his feet and asked to come forward.

The judge waved him up and Stuart followed.

"Your Honor, I have a video taken at the scene of the crime. It clearly shows Cam Derringer and Stacy Monroe shooting up the beach in Marathon."

"Yes, I've seen it. Mister Johnson, anything to add?"

"Yes, Your Honor. If we could show the film, I can show you why it isn't Cam you're seeing there but Stan Whittle, the assassin hired to frame Cam."

They went over the film as it was shown on the screen in the courtroom. Stuart pointed out the differences between Stan and me including that he was left-handed.

In the end, the judge seemed to be leaning toward the prosecution. "Cam, there is the incident with the traffic ticket," he said. "Can you explain why you would have been there?"

I thought about it again. If I said anything about being at Curt's house, it would implicate them.

"No, Your Honor," I said.

He thought about it a bit longer then said, "I don't see any other choice than to hold you on the count of seven premeditated murders."

He raised his gavel, but before he could slam it down the courtroom doors burst open and Kailey walked in.

"One minute, Your Honor," she said and came to our table.

She leaned down and told us both something that alarmed me.

"No," I said emphatically.

The doors opened again. "Too late," Kailey said.

Stacy walked into the courtroom escorted by Ryan Chase. She was wearing cuffs and carrying her laptop.

Stuart jumped up and said, "Your Honor, I believe we have further proof that Cam and Stacy were not at Sombrero Beach during the crime."

"Since this is just a hearing," the judge said, "I'll take a look."

Stacy walked forward and opened the laptop. The prosecutor and Stuart joined her at the judge's desk. Kailey also stepped forward.

"Your Honor," Kailey said, "this was taken by Stacy Monroe on the day of the crime." She hit a key and the movie started. "You can see the date and time are clearly printed at the top right corner. This is taken with Stacy's new satellite underwater camera. There is no way to alter the time or day. Here," she said, pointing to the screen, "is Cam Derringer posing in front of Joe's Barge just as they said they were."

The judge looked at the screen for a while. There were scenes where Cam was making a movie of Stacy on her first big dive.

"There is no way to alter the time and date?" the judge asked.

"No, Your Honor," Kailey said.

The judge closed the laptop and said, "Return Cam to his cell and lock Stacy Monroe up in a holding cell."

"But Your Honor," Stuart said.

"Hold your horses, Stu. I'm just going to get this checked out by a professional. If it is as it seems, they'll be free to go."

Kailey turned toward me and clapped. She already knew the answer to that question.

Four hours later, Stacy and I walked out of the courthouse holding hands. At the bottom of the steps, I hugged her and said, "That wasn't so bad," just to lighten the mood.

She looked up at me then slapped me hard across the face. I could feel it turning red.

"Every time I do anything with you, you get me into trouble. I could have spent the rest of my life in prison. You're the most irresponsible man I've ever known."

Her words hurt me more than the slap, and that was going some.

Maybe she was right. But I really couldn't see how this was my fault. Not this time. I had warned her that just being around me can be dangerous.

Barbie pulled to the curb in Stacy's car. Stacy got in and they drove away. That left me there rubbing my cheek. The jubilation I felt minutes ago was gone now. I didn't think it could ever be as good as it was when I saw Stacy set free.

I turned and walked toward home. I was supposed to call Kailey to pick me up when I was released, but I wanted to be alone. I had talked to her a few minutes earlier and she said Malinda was fully awake now and she was going to live but she'd be in the hospital for another week at least.

I walked past Betty's Bakery waved and gave her thumbs up but didn't feel like a chocolate honeybun. The only thing I could think about was finding Bexley—and a Wild Turkey.

Two blocks from the boat, I saw Stacy walking toward me. When she got to me, she stopped and took my hand. We walked to my boat without saying a word. I fixed two drinks and sat down on the chaise longue. She sat down in my lap and leaned back. We drank our drinks in silence and both fell asleep.

I didn't dream of dying or Bexley standing over me with a gun for the first time in two months.

Chapter 36

I was awoken by Walter licking me in the face. I opened my eyes and saw Diane and Kailey standing over me. I felt something move and realized that Stacy was still lying with me.

"Congratulations," Kailey said. "You did it again."

"Did what?"

"Got into trouble and got back out."

Diane chimed in, "This could have been a bad one, Cam."

"It wasn't my fault," I said, waking Stacy.

She looked up at the two women then petted Walter, closed her eyes, and went back to sleep.

Kailey said, "I know, it was my fault. I dragged you into this two months ago."

"No, you didn't. Camata did when he decided to try to kill me in Bermuda. And the gang that kidnapped Cody Paxton's fiancée tried to kill me. You were brought in by Malinda after the fact."

"I guess we shouldn't be blaming ourselves," Diane said.

"No, a guy could get slapped for that."

Stacy looked up at me and kissed me on the cheek. "Sorry about that," she said.

"So, what now?" Diane said.

"Jack and I are flying to Orlando tomorrow," I said. "We have some people to visit there."

"Who?"

"Maybe John Bexley. That's where he's from and we want to find him. This isn't over until he's gone. He probably needs to rest and that is as good a place as any."

"I'm going with you," Stacy said.

"Don't even think about it. From now on you're only with me when it's something fun and safe."

"They tried to frame me and kill me too. It wasn't just you," she said.

"I know and they're going to pay for it."

"They're?" Diane said.

Stacy and I said, "Camata," at the same time.

Kailey said, "That's my department. He'll pay for all of this, but leave him to me."

I was starting to feel a little uncomfortable now. Stacy was lying in my lap hugging me and Kailey was standing over me watching. This couldn't lead to anything that would be good for me.

I said, "Well, I guess I had better go and get the plane ready."

I started to get up, but Stacy wrapped her arms tighter. I looked up at Kailey. She smiled and asked if we'd like to be alone. I could feel my face turning red again.

Stacy looked up and realized what was going on. "Oh, I'm sorry," she said and started to get up too.

Kailey laughed. "I'm just kidding. How about another drink?"

She fixed us all another and handed ours to us. We drank and talked for a while. Stacy told me about her new adventure in diving with Kailey. "That's where I got the idea for the laptop," she said. "Kailey showed me how hers sent everything from the camera to the computer. I called Barbie to check mine and 'bingo', there it was."

"I'm very glad you figured that out. I'd still be in jail and probably prison by next year,"

"You owe me so big," she said.

"Yes, I guess I do."

"You still have to teach me how to drive my houseboat."

"When this is all over, I promise.

"Okay, now I really do have to get up. I think my leg is asleep and Walter needs to go for a run," I said.

Stacy lifted herself off me. I tried to stand, but my leg really was asleep. I rubbed it a bit and moved it around until the feeling came back.

"Old age," Kailey said.

"It can't be that. There was just a lot of weight on it."

That got me another slap from Stacy but this time on the shoulder and not so hard.

"Wanna go for a run, Walter?" I asked.

He went crazy and started running in circles.

"Get your leash," I said,

He ran to the wall and pulled his leash down. I placed it on his collar and said, "Make yourselves at home. I'll be back in twenty minutes."

"That's not a run," Stacy said.

"Walter's getting old. I don't want to wear him out."

"We'll have supper ready when you get back," Diane said.

"Sounds good."

We walked up the ramp to the parking lot where Walter stopped to do his business. I cleaned up after him and we headed out to North Roosevelt Avenue. We turned left for a block and ran up Seventh Street.

John Bexley watched Cam and his dog leave the marina and start running. He started his car and followed a block behind them. *When I find the perfect location, I'm gonna squash 'im like a bug.*

When he saw Cam turn onto Harris Avenue, he sped up. It was the perfect place to run him down. The street was empty of any other vehicles so Cam would run in the street instead of the sidewalk.

We turned onto Harris Avenue and ran down the empty street. I heard a car behind me, so I moved over closer to the curb. The sound from the car was getting louder. I could tell it was moving fast.

I glanced over my shoulder and saw that it was upon us. I jumped to the right and pulled Walter with me. The impact of hitting the curb caused me to stumble and hit the sidewalk.

I rose up to see what kind of crazy driver would do that when the car slid to a stop. I was still sitting on the sidewalk when John Bexley stepped out of his car and pointed a gun my way.

I rolled to the right behind a car as the sound of the gun hit us. Walter yelped and ran behind me. No, this wasn't his first gunfight, but this time, I had no gun. He looked at me as if to say, "Do something."

I crawled around the car. I looked both ways, but there was nowhere else to go. I was a sitting duck. I heard Bexley walking toward us.

"Well, Cam," he said. "I guess this is finally it. I've wanted this for a long time. I was afraid you were going to get stuck in prison and I'd have to have someone else kill you, but now here you are."

I looked around the ground for some kind of weapon. There was nothing. I could tell he was getting closer.

"Come on out, Cam. Let's get this over with so I can get back to the boat and kill the girls," he said, laughing.

I reached back for Walter to protect him, but he wasn't there. Did he already run away?

Then Bexley was standing over me looking down. His gun was pointed at my head. The grin on his face was pure evil. It was just like my dreams. I knew this was the end for me.

Then, with a ferocious growl and a forceful leap, Walter attacked him from behind. Bexley started flailing and swatting at the back of his leg where Walter had a good hold on him. I jumped up and threw a hard body tackle into him and took him to the ground.

Bexley was a big strong man and soon forgot about the dog. He was now pounding my face with short punches. I dropped my head so his fists would ricochet off my scull. That hurt too.

I was finally able to land a jab into his throat. He grabbed it not being able to breathe. Walter was still tearing at his leg and blood was spurting out of it. Then Bexley found his gun again and raised it toward me. I grabbed his arm and we rolled over twice before the gun went off.

It was still a few seconds before I rolled over and lay on my back. Walter was still tearing at his leg. I had felt the burn when the gun went off. I felt around my stomach and raised my head to see how badly I was hit. I only found powder wounds. I looked at Bexley. He was staring blankly at me. Walter was still biting him.

I caught my breath and said, "Walter! Stop!"

It took him a few seconds, but he let go of the leg. When I looked at him, I could see a lot of blood. "Come here, boy. Did you get hit?"

I checked him over. The blood all belonged to Bexley. I heard the sirens and saw a patrol car turn the corner. *Here we go again.*

Epilogue

I set my 241 Cessna down at the LF Wade International airport in Bermuda and taxied toward the ground transportation center.

Kailey and I were picked up there by a limousine and taken to the Loren At Pink Beach.

It was one of the most beautiful resorts I have ever seen. Our room overlooked a pool and the ocean. The restaurants were magnificent and the bars were fully stocked.

We spent three days there and I never wanted to leave. Kailey spent a part of each day doing business. She had warned me ahead of time. But when she returned in the afternoon, we'd make love and then enjoy the resort. Life was good, but I couldn't help thinking that I was only miles from Camata.

On the third day, she said, "We need to have a talk."

She told me about this plan she had been working on.

"I've been meeting with the cartel on behalf of Brittany," she said. "We've worked out a solution to our problem."

"You've been meeting with Camata?" I asked.

"No, not him, some others. I explained what would happen to them if they didn't go along with the plan."

Then she told me what was going to happen. It sounded like it could work and I was more than eager to go along with it. We went out to supper that night, came back to the room, made love, and fell asleep.

Breakfast was served in bed the next morning. "You're spoiling me," I said. "I could get used to it though."

"You ain't seen nothing yet. We have the place for another week."

We got up and showered, dressed in our casual clothing, and called the limo.

"Are you ready for this?" she asked.

"More than ready," I said and kissed her on the sidewalk outside the bar.

Kailey walked into the No Wake Bar in Bermuda. She instantly spotted Sid Camata and four of his men sitting at a table in the corner. There were two other tables with two men at each. The rest of the bar was empty.

She walked to their table watching only Camata. When he saw her coming, his laughter turned silent and he frowned.

"Hello, Camata," she said.

He only looked at her and stayed silent.

She looked at the men at the table and then around the bar. "See you guys later," she said.

Camata laughed and looked around the room. His laughter stopped again when all the men stood and walked out the door.

"Where are you going?" he yelled to them.

No one looked back at him. They all kept walking.

He turned his attention back to Kailey. "So, you think you can just walk in here and order my men around?"

Kailey looked at the bartender. "Bring him another Rum Runner. I think he's going to need it."

The bartender mixed a drink and set it on the table. Camata ignored it and kept his stare on Kailey.

"See ya around," she said and walked out the door.

"What the fuck?" Camata said.

It was my turn to walk into the bar. When Camata saw me, he stood. "What are you doing here?"

"I came to have a talk. Sit."

Camata hesitated then sat down again.

I took the chair across from him. I waved at the bartender, "Beer, please."

We were still silent when the bartender set the beer down in front of me. I picked it up and took a pull from the bottle.

"I said what the fuck are you doing here?" Camata repeated and slammed his fist on the table.

"I came to see you. Have a drink and talk about our future."

"We don't have a future," he said and downed half his drink.

"You tried to kill me again. Why do you want me dead so badly?"

"I don't like you. You shot me a few months ago while I was trying to help you."

"You were going to help me by shooting my daughter and my guest on the boat?" I said.

He laughed and rubbed his face. "I should have you killed right now. As soon as my men come back in, that's just what I am going to do."

"Your men? You don't have any men," I said and waved my hand around the room. "They're gone."

"Hector!" Camata yelled toward the door.

"Nope, no Hector. Not anymore," I said calmly.

Camata wiped his eyes and tried to get his vision clear.

"You'll pay for this," he said. "I will have you hanged."

Looking at the bartender he said, "Victor, shoot this man."

Victor said, "I don't work for you anymore. Victor Mantella works for no man." Then he folded his towel, laid it on the table, and disappeared into the back room.

"Woops," I said. "Now he's gone too."

Camata stood but lost his balance and fell back into his seat. "What the fuck did you do to me?" he said.

"Nothing, but you know I think you had one drink too many. Maybe that last one had something extra in it."

Camata looked at his glass and then back at me. "I'll kill you for…" His head hit the table with a hard thump.

I stood and walked out the door where Kailey was waiting for me. "Shall we go get something to eat?" she asked.

"Yes, that would be good. I feel a big relief. It makes me hungry."

We got into a waiting car and closed the door. I watched as the men filed back into the bar to gather their fallen leader and meet with the new head of the cartel, Victor Mantella.

The End

Don't forget to check out the Sunny Ray series. They are <u>books like no other</u>. Maybe a little too far out there for some of you but if you take a bite, I think you'll love the taste.

Meet–Wanta Mea, Youramine, Takeame, Ready, and Paris. They are a cast of characters you'll never forget.

Here is an excerpt from RUM CITY BAR.

Prologue

The doorbell rang and Rose, in her excitement of the night thinking it was one of the VIPs John was expecting, answered it without first peeking through the sidelight to see who it was.

A tall man shadowed the doorway. He had an ugly scar down the right side of his face starting at the corner of his eye and running to the tip of his chin.

Rose felt her nerves tingle and blood rush to her face.

"May I help you?" she asked, despite her eagerness to slam the door.

The man removed the old-fashioned hat he wore and took in Rose's long red hair and voluptuous body with a quick glance.

He said, "Yes. Is John in? He is expecting me."

Torn between relief and apprehension, Rose opened the door wider and invited him in. She guessed he *was* one of the VIPs.

"Have a seat, and I'll get him," she said, motioning to a rattan chair in the living room. "Who shall I say is calling on him?"

"I'll go with you if you don't mind," he said pulling a gun from inside his suit coat.

"Who was at the door?" John said as he entered the room.

The man smacked Rose, and she fell to the floor. John ran to her and helped her back to her feet.

Rose held her red cheek, and a tear ran down her face.

"What's going on here?" John said.

"My name is Don. I have come to get the million dollars you owe me," he said in a rough but calm voice.

"I don't know what you're talking about."

"The drug money you and Sunny stole from me," he said, now angered.

"It's gone. I sent it to charities," John lied.

"No, you didn't. It's in a bank account in the Grand Caymans. Transfer it to this account now, or your lovely wife dies," Don said, handing John a paper with the account number on it.

"I told you I can't do that. I don't have it."

Don pointed the gun at Rose and squeezed the trigger. There was a loud explosion, and a crimson spray covered the wall.

Chapter 65

The next evening on Rumora, we had a pig roast on the beach just steps from the bar. The music played on, and we all took turns performing our songs. I was asked to play Rum City Bar again. Halfway through the first verse, I heard another voice on stage singing along with me. I turned to see John Denver. I couldn't believe it. He was not only singing with me, he knew my song. I had cut my teeth on his songs, learning to copy his familiar licks on my guitar. Too bad, the rest of the world lost such a talent.

When the song was over, we received a standing ovation. He joined us at our table. Lori was a big fan too, and she was full of questions about how he got his inspiration for his songs.

"Life," he said, "just take the time to look around you, you'll find inspiration everywhere. In the forest, the ocean, and in space, just look up."

We did look up. It was amazing, the stars filled the sky, and we saw a shooting star running straight overhead with a tail that went from horizon to horizon.

"You did that, didn't you?" Lori said to him.

He just laughed, "I can't control the universe, but maybe God was showing off a little."

Later

Wanta Mea, Youramine, Paris, and Reddi appeared in Sunny's studio. They thought no one would see them materialize there. Sunny's mother yelled in surprise.

"Oh no, we are sorry. We didn't mean to scare you," Wanta Mea said.

"Who are you and where did you come from?" she asked.

"We are friends of Sunny's and Lori's."

I walked in the door and saw the look on everyone's faces. I started laughing.

I hope you enjoy both series. There will be more books coming in each series.